Brander Matthews

A Secret of the Sea, etc.

Brander Matthews

A Secret of the Sea, etc.

ISBN/EAN: 9783337034245

Printed in Europe, USA, Canada, Australia, Japan

Cover: Foto ©Andreas Hilbeck / pixelio.de

More available books at **www.hansebooks.com**

A SECRET OF THE SEA

A SECRET OF THE SEA

&c.

BY

BRANDER MATTHEWS

NEW YORK

CHARLES SCRIBNER'S SONS

1886

CONTENTS.

A SECRET OF THE SEA

A SECRET OF THE SEA

I.

PIRACY ON THE HIGH SEAS.

TIME was when the R.M.S. 'Patagonia' was the greyhound of the Atlantic; but that time was long past. Newer and larger boats, burning less coal and making more knots, had been built nearly every year since the 'Patagonia' had beaten the record by crossing the ocean in less than eight days from Browhead Castle to Fire Island Light. Now not only were there other deer-hounds of the deep two days faster than the 'Patagonia' had ever been, but the 'Patagonia' herself, like the man who went around the world, had lost a day. Although the 'Patagonia' had changed owners, and was now no longer a royal mail steam-ship, it had not yet fallen to the low estate of the sea-tramp, a homeless wanderer over the face of the waters, bearing hides from Buenos Ayres on one trip, and on the next carrying coals from Newcastle. She still belonged to a line in good repute, and she still made her regular round trip every five weeks from Liverpool to New York.

B 2

Thus it was that the New York newspapers had to announce one Sunday morning, after the New England spring 'had set in with its usual severity,' that the 'Patagonia' had sailed from Liverpool the day before, having on board eighty-seven first-cabin passengers and two hundred and eleven in the steerage, and bringing also 100,000*l.* in gold. In due course the 'Patagonia' ought to have arrived at Sandy Hook about ten days after she left the Mersey. Except when detained by stress of weather, the 'Patagonia' was wont to arrive off Quarantine not later than Tuesday afternoon. But on this occasion Tuesday night came, and Wednesday night, and yet the 'Patagonia' came not. It happened that the R.M.S. 'Barataria,' which was then devoting its energies to the lowering of the record, had left Liverpool an hour later than the 'Patagonia,' had waited for the mails at Queenstown, as the 'Patagonia' had not, and yet had landed its passengers on Sunday morning. Nor did the officers of the 'Barataria' report any storms which would justify the tardiness of the 'Patagonia.' It was known, however, that the missing ship was perfectly sea-worthy, and, indeed, in excellent condition, and her captain was a thorough sailor. So many little mishaps may occur to delay an ocean steamer—the bearings may get themselves overheated, or it may be necessary to stop the engines in mid-ocean to repack the steam-chest—that no anxiety was felt by the public.

Just then, indeed, the public had no attention

to spare for so slight a matter as a day's delay of
an ocean steamer, when the foundering of a Government despatch-boat nearly a fortnight before had
been followed by the fraudulent failure of a specu- ·
lative banking house, bringing down in its wake a
score of smaller concerns, including an insurance
company and a savings bank. Day after day Wall
Street trembled with the recurring shocks of failure.
The market, which before the fall of the speculative banking-house had been firm and active,
became feverish and weak; stocks began to fall
off three and four points at a drop; the boom of
Saturday gave place to a blizzard by Thursday.
While the Street was excited over the sudden col-
lapse of the great corner in Transcontinental Telegraph, the city had no time or emotion to spare on
the overdue ' Patagonia.'

When at last the ' Patagonia' did arrive, she
brought news of a sensation more startling than the
foundering of a United States despatch-boat or the
fraudulent failure of a firm of speculative bankers.
It was noon when the ' Patagonia' was sighted off
Fire Island Light, and it was late in the afternoon
before she reached her dock. Yet news flies fast,
and the latest editions of the evening papers appeared with flaming head-lines over a few brief but
double-leaded paragraphs, declaring that the most
extraordinary rumours were in circulation throughout the lower part of the city to the effect that the
' Patagonia,' which had just arrived in dock, had
been stopped off the Banks of Newfoundland by a

pirate. The officers of the 'Patagonia' were reticent.
At the office of the owners of the line the clerks
did not deny the report, but refused to give any
information. All efforts to discover the whereabouts of the captain of the 'Patagonia' had been
unsuccessful hitherto, and the reporters had been
obliged to forego the pleasure of conducting that
illegal mingling of the cross-examination and of
the examination-in-chief known as an interview.

A little before eight that evening the streets
were sprinkled with vociferant boys who rushed
about violently proclaiming an 'extra' with shrill
but not altogether articulate annunciation of its
contents. Those who were beguiled into the pur-
chasing of this catchpenny read a circumstantial
account. of the attack on the 'Patagonia' by a
Chinese dhow. The ingenious writer gave a thrilling account of the sea-fight—an account which
seemed somehow familiar to those who had once
read 'Hard Cash.' He gave precise details as to
the crew and armament of the pirate. He set
forth succinctly the piteous appeals of the purser as
the heathen Chinee removed the 100,000*l.* specie
from the strong-room of the 'Patagonia' to their
own light little skiffs. He was very dramatic in
his description of the death of the captain of the
'Patagonia,' who, so he declared, had been forced
to walk the plank—a deadly form of pedestrian
exercise much in favour among pirates, as everybody knew. This imaginative effort appeared in
the 'Comet,' a new evening journal, conducted by

Mr. Martin Terwilliger, who was formerly the editor of the New Centreville (California) 'Gazette-Standard,' and who was now trying to introduce into Eastern journalism the push and the go he had found successful in the West.

The account of the strange adventure which had befallen the 'Patagonia' printed in the New York papers of Friday morning was more sober than the highly spiced story in Mr. Terwilliger's extra, and the details given were ampler and more exact. It seems that the 'Patagonia' had had an uneventful trip, and on Saturday afternoon the passengers were looking forward to their arrival early in the week. Among the passengers were many notabilities—Judge Gillespie, Mr. Cable J. Dexter, the great Chicago grain operator, Mr. and Mrs. Eliphalet Duncan, Miss Daisy Fostelle, and her enterprising manager, Mr. Z. Kilburn. On Saturday afternoon, when the 'Patagonia' was in latitude 45° 32' and longitude 50° 28' a steamer hove in sight off the port bow. It was a long, low, rakish craft, all black. It had evidently been waiting for the 'Patagonia,' for as soon as it had had time to make sure of the 'Patagonia's' identity, it ran across her course, fired a shot across her bows, and ran up the signal Q. H., which means 'Stop; I have something to communicate.' The firing of this shot by the strange ship caused the most intense excitement and alarm on board of the 'Patagonia,' which was not allayed when the meaning of the signal was made known. While the officers of the 'Pata-

gonia' were in consultation, the stranger fired a
second shot across her bows, and ran up a second
signal, P. F.—'I want a boat immediately.' The
firing of this second shot increased the anxiety
and doubt on board the 'Patagonia.' The excited
passengers besought the officers to explain what
this meant. Experienced passengers, accustomed
to cross the ocean twice a year, declared that the
firing of a shot was a thing absolutely unheard of
except in time of war. There was an immediate
discussion as to whether war could have broken
out since the 'Patagonia' left Liverpool. An Irish
gentleman on board declared that these were the
first shots fired by the new dynamite cruiser of the
new navy of the new Irish Republic. While the
passengers were thus seeking the truth, the captain
of the 'Patagonia' had ordered her engines slowed
. down. By this time the strange ship was barely a
mile from them, and it was then easy to see many
suspicious circumstances. For one thing, not a
single member of the crew was visible. To those
with any knowledge it was plain at once that the
stranger was heavily armed, and that the single
huge gun it carried amidships, easily to be seen
from the deck of the 'Patagonia,' had range and
weight enough to sink the 'Patagonia' by a single
shot. The extreme speed of the stranger was also
apparent, as it had turned, and without difficulty it
was keeping ahead of the 'Patagonia,' and at the
same distance from her. A deputation of the passengers immediately waited on the captain to beg

him to send a boat at once, before the stranger
fired a third time. The captain had already given
orders to stop the engines and to lower a boat.
The third officer took his seat in this boat, and the
men pulled out straight for the stranger. A movement was at once visible on board the armed
steamer ; the signal flags were taken in, and a boat
was launched on the port side, out of sight from
the 'Patagonia.' This boat proved to be a gig, for
it shot around the bow of the stranger, and met
the cutter from the 'Patagonia' about a quarter of
a mile away. A communication was passed from
one boat to the other, and each pulled for its own
ship. On reaching the 'Patagonia,' the third officer
went at once to the captain's room. He bore a
sealed envelope addressed to the captain. This
address, like the letter within, was written, or
rather printed, on a type-writer. The letter was as
follows :

> S. S. 'Dare-Devil,'
> Off the Banks,
> April 1st, 1882.

Captain Riding,
    S. S. 'Patagonia,'
      Sir:

      You have on board in specie
100,000*l.* I will accept this as the
ransom of your ship. Send it to me,
20,000*l.* at a time, on five trips of your
cutter. If I do not receive the first
instalment within fifteen minutes

after you read this, I shall sink you
with a shot from my long gun.
Your obedient servant,
Lafitte,
Commanding Free Cruiser
'Dare-Devil.'

As the captain finished reading this peremptory
letter there was a sudden commotion on deck, and
one of the junior officers rushed in to report that
the stranger had raised the Black Flag. The captain stepped on deck, and with his glass easily
made out the white skull and cross-bones which
adorned the black flag flying from the peak of the
'Dare-Devil.' A thrill of horror ran through the
excited passengers. Mr. Kilburn headed a deputation which begged the captain to surrender anything and everything for the sake of saving the
lives and liberties of the passengers. Mr. Cable
J. Dexter, who had previously taken the affair as a
huge joke, read the letter from the 'Dare-Devil,' and
asked the captain if a single shot would really sink
the 'Patagonia.' The captain answered that a single
shot in the compartment amidships might sink
the ship, and that two or three shots would do it
unfailingly. 'Then,' said Mr. Dexter, 'you had
better hand over the gold. I have an engagement
in Chicago on Saturday morning, and I shall be
late for it if I have to swim ashore from here.'
Although Mr. Dexter seemed cool enough to jest,
most of the passengers were in a state of intense

excitement, and this was much increased by the announcement that the long gun on the upper deck of the 'Dare-Devil' had just been loaded, and was now trained on the 'Patagonia.'

By this time ten minutes had elapsed since the boat had returned, and suddenly a third shot from the 'Dare-Devil' ploughed the water just ahead of the 'Patagonia', and a third signal was run up, J. D. —'You are standing into danger.' Then the cap- tain yielded. The purser had already opened the strong room, and the tightly sealed, iron-strapped, hard-wood boxes of specie were at once carried on deck. Each box held 5,000*l.*, and weighed about a hundred pounds. Four of them were carefully placed in the bottom of the cutter. Fortunately there was only a light breeze, and there was no sea on at all, only the long swell always to be ex- pected off the Banks. The boat pulled for the 'Dare-Devil,' and, as before, the gig came around the bow. The transfer of the precious boxes was made as quickly and as carefully as possible. When the cutter returned for its second load, the officer reported that the three men in the gig were all masked, but that he took them for Orientals of some sort, as their hands and wrists were dark. Five times the cutter carried away four boxes, con- taining each 5,000*l.*, and five times the gig came out to receive the ransom. Before the fifth trip was completed night was falling. When the third officer reached the deck after the delivery of the final instalment of the 100,000*l.*, he took two sealed communications to the captain. Both were printed on a type-writer. One was a receipt for the gold, signed 'Lafitte.' The other was an order to the captain of the 'Patagonia' to turn on her course and to sail back toward Ireland until midnight, when she might turn and proceed again to New York. Until night made it impossible to see clearly, the passengers of the 'Patagonia' watched the 'Dare-Devil' steaming in their wake. At midnight precisely, Captain Riding changed his course and headed for New York, arriving without further adventure.

This was, in substance, the story which held the place of honour in every New York newspaper the morning after the arrival of the 'Patagonia.' And this direct statement was supplemented by numberless interviews. In the hands of men entirely great, the interview is mightier than the sword, and no more to be avoided than the pestilence which walketh in darkness. No paper succeeded in getting anything out of any of the officers, although one enterprising journal laid before its readers the *obiter dicta* of the chief steward. Several reporters succeeded in capturing Mr. Cable J. Dexter just as that great operator was checking his trunks for Chicago. At one period in his eventful career Mr. Dexter had himself been a reporter, and he surrendered himself to the inquisitors without false shame.

'I'm in a hurry, boys,' he said, 'and I really haven't any pointers to give you. Of course we

couldn't expect good luck this trip; we had four
clergymen aboard—Holy Joes, the sailors call 'em.
That's enough to make a boat snap her shaft off
short. At first I thought maybe the actors and
actresses on board would be a set-off, but it didn't
work. The pirate just broke me. Oh no: he
didn't go through me like a road-agent, but it was
just as bad. I'd been sitting with mean cards all
the afternoon, and just as the pirate fired at us I
filled a full hand—and it was a jackpot too—but
when the pirate opened, the game closed. What's
worse, I had big money up on the run, and that
damned pirate spoiled that too. I wish he'd quit
the sea and buck against the market in breadstuffs
—I'd make it hot for him!'

While certain of the passengers were wary and
fought shy of the reporters, none of the gentlemen
of the press found any difficulty in gaining admission to the presence of Miss Daisy Fostelle,
who had taken her usual spacious apartments at
the Apollo Hotel. When they sent up their cards
with a request for an interview, Mr. Kilburn, Miss
Fostelle's enterprising manager, descended to the
office to meet them, greeted them most affection-
ately, and introduced them at once with effusive
cordiality.

'I'm so very glad to be back again in America,'
said Miss Daisy Fostelle, 'though perhaps I ought
not to say that, for I had such a success in England.
I played nearly six weeks at the Royal Frivolity
theatre. Of course at first they did not quite

understand me—my style was so original, they said—so American, you know—and they did not quite know what to make of it. But I soon became a great favourite. They liked my play too ; it's the one I am to appear in here next Monday. It's called " A Pretty Girl." Oh, thank you ! It's so nice of you to say so. I had an offer to play in Paris at the Folies Fantastiques theatre — that's the best comedy theatre in Paris, you know—and they would have translated my play into French, but I was in a hurry to get back to dear old New York. Yes, the Prince of Wales was very kind indeed. He came three times to see me. Oh dear, no· I'm not going to be married—why, I'm not even engaged ! I don't see who could start such absurd rumours. You know I am wedded to my art. No, I didn't see the pirate at all, and I assure you I should not care to play the leading part in the " The Pirate's Bride." I should have hated to have been robbed of my trunks, for I have brought such lovely clothes. There is one dress made for the Empress of Austria ; oh, it's beautiful ! I shall wear it on Monday night.'

Two or three of the chiefs of the dynamite faction of the Social Anarchists threw themselves in the way of the inquiring reporters, but no definite information could be extracted from them, although they were full of vague hints and mysterious innuendoes, and let fall dark intimations that they knew all about the matter. None of the New York papers made any comment on their doubtful sayings, but the interviews with them were telegraphed to England, and called forth indignant leaders from the London journals.

The editorials of the morning papers in New York were devoted chiefly to a statement of the strangeness of the robbery. Piracy on the high seas in the nineteenth century, and within a few hours' sail of the United States, seemed like an anachronism. One paper, referring to the sinking of the Government despatch-boat, and the fraudulent bankruptcy, 'preceding a piracy as bold as any in the records of the Spanish Main,' called its able editorial 'A Carnival of Carelessness and Crime.' It suggested the immediate formation of an International League for the Patrol of the Ocean. This suggestion was accompanied by a map, and by a statistical table of the water traffic between Great Britain and the United States. Another paper had a special despatch from Washington declaring that the Secretary of the Navy would wait for further details before sending out the available vessel of the North Atlantic Squadron. A third paper came out with a quadruple sheet devoted to corporation advertising, and a series of brief biographies of the eminent pirates of the past, with outline portraits of Captain Kidd, as he sailed, and of Lafitte, the pirate of the Gulf. A stalwart organ remarked that while pirates were at large, ocean travelling could no longer be considered safe, and added that no pirate would have dared to show his face if the spirited foreign policy of Senator Doolittle had been followed up. This allowed an Independent afternoon paper to retort that as Senator Doolittle had sent a substitute to the war, it might be doubted whether even a one-armed pirate with the gout would be afraid to meet him in single combat.

But the afternoon papers contained news of more importance than this humorous expression of Independent opinion. They contained the astounding declaration that the 100,000*l* in specie which the pirate had taken from the 'Patagonia' had been returned, and was now in the possession of the agents of the line.

In company with the captain, the chief officer, and the third officer, the purser of the 'Patagonia' had gone early in the morning to the office of the agents of the line in Bowling Green. Here each of the officers told his story, which was taken down by a stenographer. As the purser was about to return to the dock, one of the clerks said, 'We have received those cases for you.'

'What cases?' asked the purser.

'The cases from Halifax,' answered the clerk.

'But I am not expecting any cases from Halifax,' was the purser's hasty reply.

'There are two cases here for you, anyhow,' said the clerk. 'They are addressed to you, they arrived this morning, and they are very heavy—as though they had machinery in them.'

The thought flashed into several minds at once

that these cases might contain infernal machines intended to destroy the office of the line, the records of the company, and the chief witnesses against the pirate. The police were notified, and in their presence the cases were opened with the greatest circumspection. The cases were found to be almost empty, except in one corner of each case, where there was a strong compartment. With redoubled care these compartments were forced open. They contained the 100,000*l* in specie, in the original tightly sealed, iron-strapped, hard-wood boxes, as addressed in England to the American consignees, whose initials and numbers they bore.

The police of Halifax were at once telegraphed to ; but the only information they could give was that the express charges had been paid by an unknown woman, who had requested that the cases be sent for. The police of New York now became as mysterious as the delegates of the Dynamite faction had been the day before. They consulted together, and allowed it to be believed that they had a clue. And there the matter rested.

The arrival of the next steamer was now awaited anxiously, to see whether it had been stopped also, or if it had at least seen any sign of the pirate. Within forty-eight hours after the unexpected and inexplicable recovery of the gold, five ocean steamers came into port. They were boarded in the lower bay by authorised reporters, but neither officers nor passengers had any information to give. They had not seen the pirate, nor

C

heard of him. Nor has the 'Dare-Devil' ever been seen again as she appeared to the anxious eyes of the passengers on the 'Patagonia.' Nor have any more orders, written on a type-writer and signed by Lafitte, been served on any steamer laden with specie.

The sudden restoration of the gold taken from the 'Patagonia,' while it increased the peculiar mystery of the affair, materially lessened the interest of those whose duty it was to hunt down the pirate. A search for the specie would have been practical, but the discovery of a pirate magnanimous enough to give up 100,000*l.* had only a speculative interest. At best it was little more than the solving of a riddle—Who was the pirate? It was but the answering of a conundrum—Why had he taken the money if he meant to return it? Men in the thick of business have no time to waste in guessing enigmas. Viewed as a whole, the robbery of the 'Patagonia,' only to return the gold, appeared purposeless. It assumed almost the form of a practical joke. To some it seemed even like a freak of insanity. Many vain efforts were made to penetrate the mystery, to guess at the pirate, and to impute a motive for his rash and reckless act; but in a few days the interest of the public began to wane, and just then it was suddenly diverted to another sensation, of more direct and personal importance to every inhabitant of the Eastern coast. A series of sharp shocks was felt by everybody on three distinct occasions. An earthquake was a novel experience to most New-Yorkers, and the reporters turned their attention at once to picturesque descriptions of effects of the visitation, and to interviews with those who had dwelt long in volcanic lands. So it came to pass that people soon ceased to puzzle themselves further about the secret of the sea.

II.

A STERN CHASE.

THERE was one person, however, who did not
allow his attention to be diverted from the strange
adventure of the 'Patagonia' by any gossip about
an earthquake. This person was Mr. Robert
White. He was a good-looking and keen-witted
young American of thirty, with straight features
and curly hair. The son of a clergyman established
over an Episcopalian church in an inland city, he
had been graduated at a fresh-water college ; but
he had always had a thirst for salt-water, and when
he came to New York to the Law School of Co-
lumbia College, he took to the water with joy. He
rowed in the Law School boat at the college
regatta on the Harlem in the spring. He did his
duty all summer on the yacht of a friend who was
fond of sailing Corinthian races. He learned
navigation, and at the school he even gave special
study to maritime law. Just as he was admitted
to the bar, his father died, leaving his little property unfortunately involved. Robert White saw
at once not only that he could no longer hope for
the assistance he would need while he was working

and waiting at the bar, but also that he must bear
part, at least, of the burden of supporting his mother
and his sister. He did not hesitate. He had edited
one of the two warring college papers ; and after he
came to New York he had written a few letters for
the chief daily of his native town. His pen was
broken to service, and he went at once to the
editor of the 'Gotham Gazette,' whom he had met
on Joshua Hoffman's yacht, and asked for work.
The editor told the city editor to do what he could
for him. The city editor sent him to interview one
of the most distinguished men of New England — a
prize-fighter, then on his first visit to New York.
The next day his assignment sent him down to
Castle Garden to sift the sensational stories of a lot
of Russian emigrants. This was not congenial
work ; but within a few weeks there was a regatta,
and it fell to him to write it up. Here was his
chance. The next morning the 'Gotham Gazette'
contained the best account of a yacht race, the
most precise and the most picturesque, which had
been printed for many a month. It made a hit,
as even the work of the anonymous reporter may
do if it is done with heart and head. It assured
his position on the 'Gotham Gazette,' which sent
him to cruise with the yacht squadron, to report
the naval review at Newport before the President of
the United States, and to give a description of the
movements of the United States Fish Commission.
To these letters his initials were attached. One of
them, a vigorous account of the showy experiments

of a torpedo-boat, attracted the notice of a sharp-
eyed editor of one of the great magazines, and he
wrote, asking if Mr. Robert White would care to
contribute three or four articles on the New England coast, to be called, 'All Along Shore,' and to
be illustrated in the highest style of American
wood-engraving.   To this pleasant task Mr. Robert
White devoted the end of summer.   When he returned to town the editor of the 'Gotham Gazette'
asked him if he would like 'to write brevier, or, in
other words, to join the editorial staff.   At the
time when the 'Patagonia' met the pirate Mr.
Robert White had been writing naval, legal, and
social editorials for several years ; his magazine
articles had appeared at last, they had been followed
by others, and they had been gathered into a handsome book, which had been well reviewed in the
leading English weeklies.   A series of sketches of
American out-door sports, signed 'Poor Bob White,'
had been very successful.   His income was not
large, but it was ample for his needs, since his
mother had died and his sister had married.   His
position was assured as one of the cleverest and
most competent of the young men who drive the
double team, journalism and literature.   He had
begun both to lay money by and to collect notes
for a real book, not a mere collection of magazine
papers : this was the 'Story of a Ship,' a history
of boats from the dug-out of the lake-dweller to
the latest device in submerged torpedo launches.
And he had done one thing more of greater im-

portance to himself than any of these—he had fallen in love.

When the meeting took place between the ' Patagonia ' and the ' Dare-Devil,' Mr. Robert White was at his native town settling his father's estate, and he did not return to New York until after the ' Patagonia ' had sailed again. He had read all the newspaper accounts and interviews with great interest. The first day after his return he went to see Mr. Eliphalet Duncan, who had been his classmate at the law school. The offices of Duncan and Sutton, attorneys and counsellors at law, were in the Bowdoin Building, No. 76 Broadway, next to those of Hitchcock and Van Rensselaer. As White went upstairs he passed a small door on which was painted ' Sargent and Co., Stock Deliveries,' and his heart gave a sudden throb, for it was Miss Dorothy Sargent, the daughter of the great speculator, that he was in love with.

' Why, Bob, how are you ? ' said Mr. Eliphalet Duncan, as his friend took a seat beside him. ' I haven't seen you since the last Judge-and-Jury dinner.'

The Judge-and-Jury was a little club to which both had belonged at the law school, and which now survived only in an annual dinner.

' I'm all right, 'Liph ; and you are too, judging by your looks. A hasty run over to Scotland and back seems to suit you. I saw you came back by the " Patagonia," and that's why I've come in to-day.'

'Your intention seems to be complimentary, but your logic is incoherent,' remarked the lawyer.

White laughed, and answered : 'I will make myself clear to the dullest comprehension.'

'Of course,' interrupted his friend.

'You know my fondness for solving problems. I always delighted in algebra at school, and I worked out the *pons* for myself. Now this unnecessary taking and giving back of the gold on the " Patagonia " strikes me as a puzzle as interesting as a man can find in a week of Sundays.'

'I doubt if you would have found it quite as interesting if you had lost a day by it,' said Duncan, dryly.

'I expect to give more than one day to it,' answered White. 'In fact, I want to stick to the case until I puzzle out the secret.'

'The detectives say they have a clue.'

'The reporter is the real detective nowadays, and as he is wont to tell all he knows, and as he has said nothing, there is, I take it, nothing known, and that leaves everything to be found out.'

'And you are going to try and to out everything ?'

'And I am going to try to find out everything —with your help.'

'For publication in the " Gotham Gazette " ?' asked the lawyer.

'For my own satisfaction first,' answered the journalist—'for the sheer enjoyment of getting at a mystery ; but, of course, in the end, if I find I have a story to tell, I shall tell it. And it seems to me that it ought not to be very hard to track the pirate to his lair.'

'I doubt if I can give you much help, but of course you are welcome to all I know.'

'The court is with you,' said White.

'I was in the main saloon, playing chess with Judge Gillespie as well as I could, while a young lady was at the piano singing "When the Sea gives up its Dead." Just as the judge mated me, we heard a shot. Going on deck, we saw the pirate, barely a mile away. I wondered why the shot had been fired, and it was not until I saw the black flag that I was willing to believe that the strange ship was a corsair. Why, I'd just as soon expected to cruise in the "Flying Dutchman" as to see a pirate—except, of course, in Penzance.'

'What was the pirate like?'

'She was a schooner-rigged steamer of perhaps three hundred tons burden, and she was a little more than a hundred feet long. She had two smoke-stacks, painted black with a red band. She rode very high out of the water, as though her bulwarks had been added to.'

'From the newspaper reports I infer that she was neither American nor English in build,' said White.

'There you are wrong, I think,' Duncan declared. 'In spite of a lateen-sail and other details, I am sure that the pirate was launched in American waters.'

'But what motive could induce an American yachtsman to turn pirate, and then to give up the proceeds of his crime?' asked White. 'Piracy on the high seas is rather a violent practical joke.'

'As to motives I can say nothing; I give you my opinion as to the facts only. In my belief the pirate was built in America. What is more, I doubt if she was as fast as the "Patagonia," and I think that we could have run away with little risk.'

'Why?'

'Because we kept gaining on her as soon as we took to our heels.'

'But a single shot from the long gun amidships would have sunk you.'

'Of course,' said Eliphalet Duncan, offering a cigar to his friend. 'I never heard of a Quaker turning pirate, but I think that was a Quaker gun!'

'What!' shouted White, in intense surprise.

'The gun fired across our bows was aimed through a port on the main-deck forward. The long gun was never fired at all, and I don't believe it could be fired. I believe it was a dummy. And that's what Judge Gillespie thinks too, and you know he is a West-Pointer.'

'A Quaker gun on a pirate!' said White, thoughtfully. 'Who ever heard of such a thing?'

'Who ever heard of a pirate's writing his messages on a type-writer?' asked Duncan.

'The presence of a type-writer on board is evidence is favour of your view that the piratical craft belongs in our own waters. The pirate of the old school might sign his own name with his own blood, but he had no use for a type-writer.'

'The making of a Quaker gun,' said Duncan, 'and the use of a type-writer, both suggest Yankee gumption. If you want to find the pirate, you need not cross the ocean. I do not know where the " Dare-Devil " went after leaving Halifax, but I feel sure that the " Dare-Devil " hailed from an American port.'

'But I see one of the accounts mentions that the crew of the gig which came out to receive the gold were Orientals,' objected White.

'That's true,' answered Duncan ; 'the third officer told me that they were Lascars, all but the man who sat in the stern-sheets.'

'And what was he ? '

'As well as the third officer could judge, he was a white man, rather portly, with bright eyes, a large nose, and a long black moustache. Apparently this man's skin was stained, for he was as dark as the Lascars, and he wore a false beard. In spite of this disguise, he impressed the third officer as a man of strong will and quick determination.'

'Proper piratical qualities.'

'Of course,' assented Duncan.

'Do you think this man with the stained face, the long moustache, and the false beard was the pirate chief, the new Lafitte ?' asked White.

'That was my impression,' answered Duncan. 'It seems to me very probable that the head which had planned the robbery should personally see to the delivery of the treasure.'

'That brings up again the chief puzzle—why did he take the gold if he meant to give it up, and why did he give it up after running the risk of disgrace and death to get it? This is the main question. It is more important to get an answer to that than to identify the man or the ship, or rather to find a motive of this apparently motiveless act will be to have gone far toward the discovery of the man himself.'

'As for motives,' said Duncan, 'there are a plenty.'

'Such as—— ?'

'I mean that there are possible explanations in plenty of these proceedings. Perhaps the man was mad : there is a simple explanation.'

'A little too simple, I fear : marine kleptomania is not an accepted plea as yet,' said White.

'A madman may have great cunning and persistence,' urged Duncan. 'Or the man may have been sane but fickle, and after the robbery he quietly changed his mind.'

'That is rather a strain on our credulity, isn't it?' queried White.

'It is improbable, but it may be the fact, for all that. Then, again, perhaps the mate of the " Dare-Devil " experienced a change of heart, and repented of his piracies, and converted the rest of the crew, and got them to mutiny, whereupon they made Mr.

Lafitte walk the plank, after which they returned the gold, and then they scuttled the ship.'

White smiled, and said, 'I see Lascars giving up gold and scuttling a ship.'

'It would be a pity to think that so pretty a yacht had been sent to the bottom.'

'So you think the pirate was a yacht?'

Duncan hesitated a moment, and then answered: 'What else could she be? Plainly enough she was not a Government gun-boat, and as plainly she was not a boat built for freight or passengers; she had no hold for the one, and no accommodation for the others. What could she be but a pleasure-boat?'

'But a yacht has not high bulwarks or two smoke-stacks,' objected White.

'Of course there had been an attempt to disguise her. I think the bulwarks were part of the disguise; and perhaps the second smoke-stack was too, although that had not struck me before.'

'Then,' said White, 'in your opinion, the "Dare-Devil" is an American steam-yacht of perhaps three hundred tons, and about a hundred feet long?'

'It is unprofessional to give an opinion without a retainer,' answered the lawyer, smiling, 'but you have expressed my private views with precision and point.'

'The witness may stand down,' said the journalist, rising. 'Having inserted the corkscrew of interrogation, and extracted the pure wine of truth,

I have no further use for you.   Now I must tear
myself away.'

'Come in and dine with us quietly one night
next week.   Mrs. Duncan will be glad to see you.'

'I'd like to do it, but I have no time.   You see,
I have been away for a fortnight, and I'm in arrears
with my work.'

'Make it Tuesday, and you will meet Miss
Sargent,' urged Duncan.

'Tuesday?' said White, as his pulse quickened.
'I think, perhaps, I could manage it on Tuesday.'

'Then we shall expect you at half-past six.
There'll only be four of us.   You know Miss
Sargent, I think.'

'Oh yes, I know her,' answered White, as
lightly as he could.

'A charming girl—isn't she?' asked Duncan.

'She is, indeed,' said White, with perhaps more
warmth than was absolutely necessary.

'She is a great friend of my wife's,' said Duncan
—and White envied Mrs. Duncan—'and she's
always at our house'—and then White envied
Duncan.   To hear her name was a delight, and to
talk about her was a delicious torture.   After a
moment's silence he said,

'I see her father's office is just under you.'

'Oh yes, Sam Sargent has his head-quarters
here.   I don't know whether you like that man,
Bob, or not?'

'I do not know him,' answered White, uneasily.

'Well, I know him, and I detest him.   Whenever I see him and think of his daughter, then I know his wife must have been an angel from heaven.'

'You are a little rough on him, 'Liph,' said White, deprecatingly.

'No, I am not. She has an air of breeding, and she carries herself like a lady, but her father is not a gentleman—at least—you know what I mean. The man is coarse-grained, in spite of all his smartness and brilliancy. You have only to look in his face to see that. He took up the right trade when he turned gambler.'

'Gambler?'

'Of course. Stock speculator, if you like that term better. Speculating in stocks is not business ; it is gambling. The money made in speculating is not business earnings, whatever it may pretend to be ; it is winnings, no more and no less. I don't object to a game of poker now and then myself, but when I win thirty or forty dollars I don't put the sum down in my books as earnings. Now it is men like Sam Sargent who have confused and corrupted the public mind in regard to this thing. They are gamblers, but they masquerade in the honourable garb of business men. And he has the impudence to want to go into politics.'

'He is no worse than the rest,' ventured White apologetically.

'Of course,' retorted Duncan, promptly ; 'and he's no better. And he'll come to grief, like the rest of them. Only a few days ago he had a very tight squeeze, so Mat Hitchcock tells me.'

'How so?'

'He was caught in the Transcontinental Telegraph corner, and he would have lost all he had left, and more too, if this brief panic had not come to his rescue, and knocked the bottom out of the market. It was this fraudulent bankruptcy and the failures it caused which saved Sam Sargent.'

'You do not like him?' said White, smiling.

'But I like his daughter,' answered Duncan.

'So do I,' replied White as cheerfully as he could.

'Of course,' said Duncan; 'and we shall expect you on Tuesday.'

'You may rely on me;' and White shook hands with Eliphalet Duncan and withdrew. As he reached the foot of the stairs, opposite to the office of Sargent and Co., the door opened, and a customer came out, pausing on the threshold to ask, 'When do you expect Mr. Sargent back?' White could not help hearing the answer: 'He'll be here in a week or two. You know he is at Bermuda, on the "Rhadamanthus," with old Joshua Hoffman.' White knew that Joshua Hoffman was one of the most distinguished citizens of New York—a man who had made a fortune, which he administered for the public good as though he was not the owner, but only a trustee for the poor and the struggling.

'If Sam Sargent is off on a cruise with Joshua Hoffman,' thought the young man who was in love with Sam Sargent's daughter, 'why, he can't be quite as black as 'Liph paints him.'

It was on Friday that Robert White had called on Eliphalet Duncan, and he gave most of Saturday also to the pursuit of the pirate. He had a long talk with Judge Gillespie, who confirmed all that Duncan had said. The so-called 'Dare-Devil' was probably an American steam-yacht of three hundred tons or thereabouts. Now there were five or six yachts on the American register which answered fairly enough to the description of the 'Dare-Devil,' after making due allowances for the efforts to disguise her. But all of these—except two— were easily accounted for, and must be unhesitatingly ruled out, as they were not in commission. Of the two American steam-yachts approximately like the 'Dare-Devil,' one, the 'Pretty Polly,' belonged to a wealthy clergyman, and was then in the Mediterranean, cruising along the Holy Land with a full ship's company of missionaries ; the other was at Bermuda—it was the 'Rhadamanthus,' and it belonged to the good Joshua Hoffman.

When, by a process of exhaustion, as the logicians call it, Mr. Robert White had arrived at this useless result, it was late on Saturday afternoon, and he looked back along the week, and he felt that it had been well-nigh wasted. He had not made any progress toward the solution of the problem of the piracy against the 'Patagonia,' and he had not seen Miss Dorothy Sargent.

III.

TAKING SOUNDINGS.

ROBERT WHITE had met Miss Dorothy Sargent
for the first time late in the preceding fall. Mrs.
Eliphalet Duncan, who was always getting up
something new, got up a riding party to go together to Yonkers for a light dinner, and to ride
back to the city by the light of the autumn moon.
As the merry cavalcade set forth Mrs. Duncan
introduced Mr. White to Miss Sargent, by whose
air of distinction, as she sat firmly on a high-spirited
bay mare, he had been attracted already. Her
manner, like her simple habit, which fitted her
slight figure to perfection, was quiet and unobtru-
sive ; and she had in abundance that indefinable
but unmistakable quality called style. Her light
golden hair was tied in a neat knot under her tall
hat, and a semicircle of veil half hid her face, although a bright glance from her frank blue eyes
passed without difficulty through the filmy barrier
as Mrs. Duncan presented White to her. This
glance, the merry smile which occasioned it, the
ray of the afternoon sun as it made molten the
twisted gold of her hair, the gentle dignity of her

attitude—these united in a picture which printed itself indelibly in White's memory.

Before they had passed the reservoir in Central Park White had discovered that Miss Sargent rode well, like one with a strong natural gift of horsemanship, well developed by an intelligent master. As they cantered side by side through the russet bowers and leaf-strewn lanes of the park, he could not but notice how perfectly her exquisite American grace seemed to harmonise with the soft and delicate hues of the fading landscape, as the glory of the American autumn was fast departing. He marked how her colour rose with the Amazonian enjoyment, with the honest delight of the genuine horsewoman, and he wondered how she came by her beauty. He was vaguely familiar with the features of her father, one of the best-known men about town, and he knew that Sam Sargent was an operator in stocks and a fellow of bluff joviality, hail-fellow-well-met with most men, getting the utmost possible sensual enjoyment out of life, and having no sympathy at all with plain living and high thinking.

There was no lack of candidates for the place by Miss Sargent's side as the little party rode forth, or as it rode back again by the full light of a glorious moon ; but White set his wits to work, and managed to monopolise her company the whole of the long blissful afternoon and the happy, evening—all too short. Before they reached the park on their return he was on the verge of

wishing that her lively mare would try to run away
or to throw her, or to do anything that would give
him a chance to show his devotion.   When at last
he had helped her to dismount and had said good
night, he felt lifted out of himself, and as though
intoxicated by some mysterious but delicious elixir.
He was in love ; and the thought of his own un-
worthiness brought him back to earth, and kept
him awake a good part of the night.

As it began, so it went on all winter.   White
discovered where she went to church, and he
walked home with her on Thanksgiving morning,
learning that her father rarely ventured within the
sacred edifice except when some famous pulpit
orator came to preach a charity sermon.   On
Christmas Day he sat in a pew where he might
gaze his fill upon her, and his heart overflowed
with peace and good-will.   Mrs. Duncan—just
before she made her hurried trip to Europe—asked
a little party to see the old year out and the new
year in, and as White kept as close as he could to
Dorothy the new year began for him with joy and
gladness.   Mrs. Duncan's sister-in-law, Mrs. Sutton,
kept Twelfth Night with due celebration of the
ancient rites of that honourable feast.   Chance
crowned White king, and of course he chose
Dorothy for his queen.   He noticed that her face
flushed with pleasure as he took her by the hand.
But before the evening was over he began to
wonder how he had displeased her, for of course
he could not think her capricious.   When next

they met she was cold toward him, and he suspected she had avoided him. On St. Valentine's
Day he mustered up courage and sent her a tall
screen of growing ivy, in the centre of which
clustered a bunch of uncut Jacqueminot roses in
the shape of a heart. For this she thanked him in
a clever little note, as distant as it was kindly. He
wondered whether she guessed that he loved her,
and sought to discourage him.

This was the state of affairs between them when
they sat opposite to each other at one of those exquisite little dinners for four which Mrs. Duncan
was famous for. There was a dim, religious light
in the Duncans' dining-room befitting the mystic
rites of gastronomy. As White looked up and
caught Dorothy's eye he wondered whether the
faint flush which spread over cheek and throat in
such becoming fashion was really a blush, or
whether it was due only to the red silk shades on
the tall candles at the corners of the table.

'I see the eye of the law upon me, Mr. White,'
she said, gaily. 'What will the verdict be?'

'You deserve to be drawn and quartered, Dora,'
interjected Mrs. Duncan, 'for keeping us waiting
seven minutes. Fortunately I knew your ways,
and allowed ten.'

'Why is it you are always seven minutes late?'
asked Duncan. 'You have nothing to do.'

'Nothing to do? Well, I like that!' began
Dorothy.

'Of course,' said Duncan, maliciously. 'I

think I should like having nothing to do myself
—for a little while.'

'That's just like a man!' retorted the young
lady. 'I'm sure I've done more than you have.
I've been to cooking school, and I have had an
Italian lesson, and I've practised two hours, and
I've been shopping, and I've paid ten visits, besides
keeping house, which is work enough for one able-
bodied woman.'

'Indeed it is,' interrupted Mrs. Duncan, whose
household was organised to run like clock-work,
and who never heard from it except when it
struck.

'My father never scolds,' continued Miss Sargent, 'but he depends on me to make him comfortable. I don't know what he'd do without
me.'

'He has to do without you when you dine out,'
said Duncan slyly.

'Oh, then I send him off to the club—and he
goes like a lamb! Why, in the three weeks before
Lent he dined at home only once.'

'Was he invited out?' asked Duncan.

'No; but I was,' she answered frankly. 'He
used to meet Mr. Thursby at the club, and they
dined together.'

'Dick Thursby?' asked Mrs. Duncan.

'Yes. My father's very fond of him—he says
he's a man of a thousand.'

'He's a man of a good many thousands, if
report can be believed,' said White, remembering

with a sudden sinking of the heart that rumour reported this Mr. Thursby as very devoted to Miss Sargent.

'His wife left him a lot of money,' said Duncan.

'And her mother has never forgiven him for taking it,' added Mrs. Duncan. 'She abuses him dreadfully.'

'No man is a hero to his mother-in-law,' said White, lightly. He was afraid of Thursby, but he was not willing to say anything against him.

'That's not because he may not be a hero,' suggested Dorothy, 'but rather because she is a mother-in-law.'

'I hear he is beginning to take notice again,' remarked Mrs. Duncan.

'He's been flirting outrageously with that Hitchcock girl all winter,' said Dorothy.

'Dear me,' said Mrs. Duncan, slyly, 'I thought he had been very attentive to you.'

'I never noticed that,' laughed Dorothy, as White moved uneasily. 'The only things I did notice about him were that he had a large mouth, and that only very small talk fell from it.'

'Then you are not setting your cap for him?' said Duncan, inquisitively.

'Do you think I am a young lady with all the modern improvements ready to marry any goose if he has golden eggs?'

'I will not discuss the point with you,' said Duncan. 'I never care to argue at dinner; the

one who is not hungry always gets the best of
it.'

White breathed more freely when he heard her
treat his rival thus scornfully.

'I did not think Mr. Thursby was an unintelli-
gent man,' said Mrs. Duncan; 'he was in Congress for a year or two.'

'Why didn't he serve his full term?' asked
White, unable to resist the chance. 'Was he
pardoned out?'

'Mr. White'—and Miss Dorothy's voice was
very mischievous—'when you speak slightingly of
Congress, perhaps you forget that my father has
political aspirations.'

'I assure you I did not know it,' and poor
White blushed scarlet at his blunder.

'Mr. Joshua Hoffman has been urging my
father to go to Congress for a long while.'

'Joshua Hoffman's help is worth having,' remarked Duncan, as he tasted his champagne, 'no
matter whether what you want is in this world or
the next.'

'It is delightful to see how all classes respect
and honour Hoffman's goodness,' added White.
'He's one of the few men who belong to the
Church and who do not act as though the Church
belonged to them.'

'He's had a great fancy for my father,' said
Dorothy, 'ever since my father gave him Jean-
nette J.'

'He ought to be grateful for one of the finest

and fastest horses on the track,' answered White,
' although he never bets on her or lets her trot for
money.'

' Isn't your father off with Joshua Hoffman
now ?' asked Mrs. Duncan.

' Oh yes ! they are at Bermuda. They went
on the " Rhadamanthus." '

White suddenly remembered that Joshua
Hoffman's yacht was the only ship he had been
able to find resembling the ' Dare-Devil.'

' At least my father went on her—Mr. Hoffman
was delayed at the last moment, and had to wait
over for the regular steamer.'

' Is he on the " Rhadamanthus " now ?' queried
White.

' Oh yes, he is there *now*. But my father had
to go down all alone. He didn't mind that, as the
sailing-master of the " Rhadamanthus " is a great
friend of his. He'd do anything for my father ; I
heard him say so once.'

' Perhaps Mr. Sargent got him his berth ?' suggested White, strangely interested in the topic, as
he was in anything which might bear, however
remotely, on the mysterious pirate.

' I believe he did,' replied Dorothy ; ' but
Captain Mills owed my father a great deal before
that. At least I think so. I suppose I might as
well tell the whole story. It's not much, either.
But one summer, several years ago, I had been
asleep in a hammock on the piazza, and I waked
up just in time to hear Captain Mills say : " I owe

you more than I can ever pay, Mr. Sargent. You
have done more than save my life. Talk is cheap,
but I hope some day I may be able to show you
that I do not forget." '

'And what did your father say to that?' asked
Mrs. Duncan.

'Well, you know his jocular way. He said,
"That's all right, captain; first time I want a man
stabbed in the back, Italian fashion, I'll let you
know." And Captain Mills took my father's hand
and said, very seriously, "You may joke, Mr. Sargent, but I mean what I say, and, short of murder,
I don't believe there's anything I'd stick at to do
you a good turn." '

'It's lucky your father isn't a bold bad man,'
said Duncan, 'or he might get Captain Mills to
scuttle the ship, or to splice the main brace, or to
do any of the wicked things that sailor-men delight in.'

'Don't you be too sure of my father,' Dorothy
answered, gaily. 'He often says that if he wasn't
on the Street he'd like to be a pirate!'

'Indeed!' ejaculated White, earnestly.

'He has a whole library of books about pirates,
but he says that the best of them all is a brief
biography of Blackbeard, which he found his
office-boy reading.'

'Of course he took it away from the office-boy,
and scolded him,' remarked Duncan, 'and then
went into his private office and devoured it
himself?'

'That's just what he did,' answered Dorothy, 'and he says it is the most expensive book in his library now, for while he was reading it the market went up or down, or something, and he lost a chance of making several thousand dollars.'

'Piracy is a losing business nowadays,' said White.

'Of course,' added Duncan, quickly. 'A brave man can do better now-a-days in Wall Street than on the Spanish Main.'

'I have always heard Captain Mills well spoken of,' remarked White.

'Oh, he's a fine man!' said Dorothy, enthusiastically. 'And I am so glad he is in charge of the "Rhadamanthus," now that Mr. Hoffman has a crew of Lascars.'

'Lascars?' said Duncan and White together, looking at each other.

'Yes; he shipped them a few weeks ago, when he was in the Mediterranean.'

'Joshua Hoffman does have the oddest notions,' said Mrs. Duncan.

'Of course,' remarked her husband; 'he has very queer kinks in him. But he is a good man and an honourable man, and the whole country is proud of him and of his work.'

The conversation thus directed to Joshua Hoffman's characteristically American career was enlivened by many anecdotes of his poverty in youth, of his shrewdness in business, of his simple and straightforward integrity, and of his thoughtful

and comprehensive charity. Then the talk turned
to other topics as the perfectly served dinner
pursued its varied courses. At last came coffee.
The two ladies rose and took their tiny cups into
the parlour, leaving the two men to smoke their
cigars in the dining-room. But Robert White lent
little attention to Duncan's shrewd and pleasant
chat when Dorothy Sargent followed Mrs. Duncan
across the parlour to the piano, and began to sing.
She had a light, clear, soprano voice, sufficiently
well trained, and she sang without effort, and as
though she enjoyed it.

After she had sung two or three songs Mr.
Duncan called out from the dining-room, 'Now
Miss Dorothy, by request——'

'Oh, I know what you want,' she interrupted,
gaily.

'Of course,' said Duncan, lighting a second
cigar. His Scotch ancestors had died for the
Stuarts, and he thrilled with hereditary loyalty as
Miss Sargent sang 'Here's a health of King
Charles,' with a dramatic intensity for which the
careless observer would never have given her
credit.

As Robert White rose to join the ladies, the
butler told Mr. Duncan that a gentleman wanted
to see him.

'Close the doors leading into the Japanese
room,' said Duncan, 'and show the gentleman in
here.'

The room between the parlour and the dining-

room Mrs. Duncan had decorated in the Japanese
style. The walls were covered with Japanese
paper and hung with plaques of *cloisonné*. The
furniture was of bamboo with cushions of Japanese
embroidery. Japanese lanterns, dexterously arranged for gas, shed a gentle light. Although the
room was probably hopelessly incorrect in the
eyes of a Japanese—had Mrs. Duncan had one on
her visiting list—the effect was novel, and exotic
and charming.

White passed through this room, and joined
Miss Dorothy at the piano. He turned the leaves
for her as she sang 'The Shepherd's Hour.' He
thought she had never looked so lovely, and he
knew he had never loved her as much. He felt
that the time had come when he must put his fortune to the touch, when he must learn whether life
was to be happiness or misery. When she finished
the song she left the piano hastily, and begged
Mrs. Duncan to play. White seconded her. Mrs.
Duncan was an admirable pianist, but she was a
match-maker even more accomplished.

'I'll play,' she said, 'on one condition only:
you two must go into the Japanese room and
talk.'

'Talk while you are playing?' protested
Dorothy.

'Yes,' answered Mrs. Duncan firmly. 'You
need not talk loudly, but you must talk: then I
shall not feel as though I were giving a concert.'

'If we must, we must,' said Dorothy; and she

took a seat in the Japanese room. White sat himself down on a stool at her feet, as Mrs. Duncan began one of Mendelsshon's 'Lieder ohne Worte.'

'How lovely those songs without words are!' said Dorothy, after a silence which threatened to become embarrassing.

'How lovely it would be,' answered White, 'if we could express ourselves without words, if we could only set forth without speech the secret thoughts and feelings of our souls!'

'Do you really think so?' asked Dorothy. 'Sometimes it would be very awkward, I fear.'

'Surely you would not mind letting the whole world read your innocent heart?'

'Indeed I should,' cried Dorothy. Why, there are things I shouldn't like anybody to know.'

Robert White noticed the sudden blush which accompanied these words. In his eyes her delightful alternations of colour were perhaps her greatest beauty.

'I wish you could know without my telling what my heart is full of just now,' he said, controlling his voice as best he could.

The colour fled from her cheek, and left it as white as marble. With a little effort, she said, 'How do I know that it would interest me?'

'Don't you take any interest in me?' asked White.

'Indeed I do, Mr. White, but——'

'Then you must have seen that I love you,' he interrupted, unable to refrain any longer. 'Don't tell me that you have not seen it. Don't tell me that my love is hopeless.'

The colour came back slowly to her face and neck, and she said, shyly, 'I do not tell you that, because it would not be true.'

'Then you do love me?'

'Just a little bit.'

He clasped her in his arms, as Mrs. Duncan turned over her music and played a nocturne of Chopin's.

They talked on in perfect bliss for a few minutes, then she said, suddenly, 'But you must speak to my father.'

'I will ask him five minutes after he sets foot on shore.'

'He will never consent,' continued Dorothy. 'He has always said he could never let me go, and I have always promised never to leave him.'

'But that was before you gave yourself to me,' said her lover.

'I suppose so, but I don't know what he will do without me.'

'Just think how I have done without you all these years. It's my turn now.'

'He has been so good to me always.'

'I will be so good to you always. How could I be anything else?'

She looked at him, and he leaned forward and kissed her softly.

'But I will never marry you without his consent,' she said.

Just then Eliphalet Duncan threw open the folding doors of the dining-room, and announced to Miss Dorothy that her maid and her coupé had come to take her home. As White rose to see her into the carriage, Duncan asked him to come back a minute after Miss Sargent was off, as he had something to tell. White waited in the hall while the maid bundled Dorothy up in her fleecy wraps. Then he helped her into her carriage. The sharp eyes of the maid were on him, and he could say nothing. He gave her hand a precious squeeze as she said 'Good-night.'

'May I see you to-morrow?' he asked.

'Yes, to-morrow,' she answered ; and with this word of promise and hope they parted.

White went up to Duncan's study.

'Who do you suppose my visitor was?' asked Duncan.

'How should I know?' asked White.

'He's as anxious as you to find out who the pirate was that stopped the "Patagonia." He was one of our passengers. · And he came to tell me a curious discovery of his. He is interested in a type-writer manufactory, and he noticed certain peculiarities in the notes which the pirate sent. As soon as he arrived here he set to work investigating. He has found out that the type-writer used by the pirate is one of a new style just put out by the company in which he is a shareholder. This new style was for sale only a month ago. Very few of them were sold before the First of April—the day when the pirates made fools of us.'

'Has he a list of the purchasers?' asked White, anxiously.

'His list is incomplete, but among those who bought this new style of type-writer was Joshua Hoffman.' .

'The owner of the "Rhadamanthus"?' inquired the astonished White.

.'Of course,' said Duncan.

IV.

IN THE PIRATE'S LAIR.

To any one not accustomed to the sharp contrasts of American life it would have seemed impossible that Miss Dorothy Sargent should be the daughter of Mr. Samuel Sargent. She was slight and graceful, delicate and ethereal, as is the wont of the American girl. He was solid and florid ; he was a high liver and of a full habit. His eye was very quick and sharp, as though it was always on the main chance, but there was generally to be seen a genial smile on his sensual mouth, not altogether hidden by a heavy moustache. He was at once a very smart man and a very good fellow. His friends often referred to the magnetism of his manner. He was kindly, generous, shrewd, and unscrupulous. Moralities differ, and Sam Sargent had the morality of Wall Street, and he knew no other : he would engineer a corner without a thought of mercy ; but he never ' went back ' on his bank, and he never ' lay down ' on his broker ; and these are the cardinal virtues in the Street. According to his lights, he was an honest man, but he wore his principles easily, and he had cultivated his senses at the expense of his conscience.

His father had skimped and scraped for years that the son might go to college, and was now living in restful happiness on a big farm near his native town—a farm bought for him by his successful son. The college allowed its poorer students to pay their way by manual labour, and most of the shelving and other carpenter-work in the college library had been done by Sam Sargent, who had since endowed the library with twenty-five thousand dollars. After he left college he edited a country weekly for two or three months; then he turned auctioneer; after that he was advance agent for a small circus; then the war broke out, and he raised a company, and rose to be colonel of volunteers. Wounded and sent home on a furlough, he delayed his return from Washington to his Western home long enough to marry the most beautiful daughter of one of the proudest of the first families of Virginia. After helping to convert the steamers on the Upper Mississippi into home-made ironclads, he resigned, and became interested in various Government contracts. He did his duty by the Government, and made money for himself. He put his earnings into the little local railroad of his native place. When the war was over, and the railroads of the West began to be consolidated and to push across the plains and the mountains, the little road of which Sam Sargent was president was wanted by two rival systems. Sam Sargent sold to the highest bidder, after judiciously playing one against the other; and he brought his money and

E 2

his experience to Wall Street.   A man cannot run
with the hare and hold with the hounds ; on the
Street a new-comer is either a wolf or a lamb : Sam
Sargent was not a lamb.   In the uneasy and restless turmoil of the Stock Exchange he was in his
element, and there he thrived.   Every summer,
when stocks were sluggish or stagnant, the speculator sought other forms of excitement.   One
year he hired a fast yacht, and the next he bought
a pair of fast trotters.   One summer he let his
fondness for poker run away with him, and he was
a player in the famous game which lasted two days
and three nights : at the end of the second day he
had lost $150,000, but during the last night he won
it all back, and $65,000 besides.   No man could
deny his quickness, his coolness, or his nerve.   Of
late he had begun to take an interest in politics,
and he was known to be seeking a nomination for
Congress from one of the brown-stone districts :
the machine of his party was all ready to work in
his behalf.   To attain to this honour was his one
unsatisfied desire, and his heart was set on it.

About three weeks after the ' Patagonia ' had
been robbed off the Banks by the ' Dare-Devil,' Mr.
Joshua Hoffman's yacht, the ' Rhadamanthus,' returned to New York from Bermuda, bringing back
Mr. Sam Sargent and Mr. Joshua Hoffman himself.   Among the letters which Sargent found on
the table of his handsome private office in the
Bowdoin Building, No. 76 Broadway, overlooking
a part of Trinity Churchyard, was one from Robert

White, requesting an immediate interview on a matter of the highest importance. Sargent knew White's name as a rising young literary man, he had heard his daughter speak of meeting White, and he was aware of White's connection with the ' Gotham Gazette.' He wrote Mr. White a polite note, saying that he should be glad to see him the next day at three.

Precisely at three the next afternoon, as the bells of Trinity rang the hour over the hurrying heads of the sojourners in Wall Street, Robert White handed his card to the office-boy of Sargent and Company, and was shown at once into the private office of the special partner. Sargent rose to receive him, saying, ' I'm glad to make your acquaintance, Mr. White. There is a comfortable chair. What can I do for you to-day ? '

As he said this he gave White a look which took him in through and through. White felt that Sargent had formed at once an opinion of his character, and that this opinion was probably in the main accurate. ' Are we alone,' he asked, ' and secure from interruption ? '

Sargent stepped to the door and said to the attending office-boy, ' If anybody calls, just say I have gone.' Then he closed the door and turned the key in the lock. Taking his seat at his desk, he said, ' Now, Mr. White, I am at your service.'

' As I wrote you, Mr. Sargent, I desire a few minutes' talk with you on a matter of great importance,' began White.

'Excuse me a moment,' interrupted Sargent, taking a box of cigars from a drawer in his desk. 'Do you smoke?'

White declined courteously.

'I trust you will excuse me if I light up?'

'Certainly,' said White.

'I never smoke during business hours,' explained Sargent, 'but at three I always indulge myself in a little nicotine.'

White noticed that under cover of the first two or three puffs of smoke the speculator gave him a second penetrating examination. The journalist knew that his task was difficult enough at best, and this little manœuvre seemed to double the difficulty. But his voice did not reveal this feeling as he said :

'The business I have to speak about, Mr. Sargent, is as private as it is important. I am aware that for a moment I may seem to you to be prying, not to say impertinent. I beg to assure you in advance that such is not my intent. If you will bear with me until I am done, I think you will then pardon my apparent intrusion.'

'Fire away,' said Sargent, blowing a series of concentric rings of smoke, 'and put the ball as close to the bull's-eye as you can.'

'What I desire to talk about is the taking of 100,000*l.* in specie from the "Patagonia" on the afternoon of the First of April.'

'Indeed?' queried Sargent, sending forth a final ring of smoke as perfect as any of its predecessors.

'And pray what have I to do with that little speculation in gold?'

'At the time that money was taken you were
short of Transcontinental·Telegraph stock, and
you stood to lose nearly half a million dollars.'

'If you had not warned me that you would be
intrusive, I think I should have been able to discover it for myself.'

'Hear me out.'

'I do not see any connection between my
private affairs and the "Patagonia" adventure. But
go on.'

White continued in the calm voice he had
maintained from the beginning of the interview:

'Before that gold could be landed in Nova
Scotia there had been a panic here in Wall Street,
the bottom had dropped out of Transcontinental
Telegraph, your partners had covered your shorts,
and you were in a fair way to make a good profit.'

'Well?' asked Sargent, quietly.

'Well—then the gold from the "Patagonia" was
restored to its owners.' As he said this, White
watched Sargent closely. A second series of
vortex rings was in process of construction. Suddenly Sargent turned slightly, and looked White
full in the face.

'Mr. White, it is evident that you do not know
me. I am a bad man to bluff. I do not choose
to understand you insinuendoes, as the darkey
called them——'

'I made no insinuations.'

'You have been dropping mysterious hints,' said Sargent, firmly.

'If you have picked them up, why——'

'Just let me tell you, Mr. White, that if you pick me up for a fool, you will lay me down again like a red-hot poker. I see you are driving at something. Now just stop this feeling over the surface and cut to the quick. If you have anything to say, say it out and be done with it.'

'I can put the matter in a nutshell, if you will give me five minutes,' said White, quietly.

'Load your nutshell and touch off the fuse,' answered Sargent, settling back comfortably in his chair.

'My chain is not quite complete, I confess,' began White; 'there are several slight links wanting. But it is strong enough. Here is my story: When the "Patagonia" sailed from Queenstown with 100,000*l.* on board, you were in urgent need of about $500,000. Owing to the unexpected detention of Mr. Joshua Hoffman in this city, you were the sole passenger on the "Rhadamanthus" when she cleared from New York for Bermuda. The crew of the "Rhadamanthus" were Lascars. The captain was under great obligations to you, and would do anything for you.'

Here White remarked that Sargent gave him a quick look as who should say, 'How came you to know that?'

'Instead of going directly to Bermuda, you made for the Banks of Newfoundland. On the voyage up you rigged a false funnel on the "Rha-damanthus," you built false bulwarks, and you mounted a Quaker gun amidships.'

Again White caught the same quick look, as though Sargent, in spite of his self-control, was surprised at the accuracy of White's information.

'You arrived off the Banks just in time to intercept the "Patagonia." You fired across her bows with the little gun of the yacht. You pretended to load the Quaker gun. You sent a message to the captain of the "Patagonia"—a message written by a type-writer bought by Joshua Hoffman the day before the yacht sailed. You stained your face and put on a false beard, and you yourself sat in the stern-sheets of the gig which was rowed out to receive the gold. When you left the "Patagonia," as night fell, you steamed straight for the little place which Captain Mills owns on the coast of Nova Scotia near Halifax. You landed the gold at his private dock by night: fortunately for you, no custom-house official caught sight of you. Whether you had intended to take the gold and fly, or whether you meant to use it to pay your losses in the Transcontinental Telegraph corner, I do not know. But when you touched land you got the news of the panic here, and of the fall in the price of Transcontinental Telegraph. No longer needing the money, you determined to return it, and to let the affair pass off as a practical joke appropriate to the First of April. Mrs. Mills took the cases to Halifax, and saw that they were forwarded

to New York. Then you took the yacht to Bermuda
as fast as she could steam, getting there long
before Mr. Joshua Hoffman arrived on the regular
steamer. No one in Bermuda connected the " Rhadamanthus " with the " Dare-Devil," because no one
knew anything about the temporary robbery of the
' Patagonia' until the arrival of the mail. There is
no telegraph to Bermuda. The gold having been
returned to its owners, you thought there would
be no motive for pursuit and for prosecution.
You believed that the whole matter would blow
over, and that long before you got back to New
York people would have something else to talk
about than the adventure of the " Patagonia." For
further safety you have persuaded Mr. Joshua Hoffman to send the " Rhadamanthus " to Rio Janeiro
to bring back the boy-naturalist who has been
making collections along the Amazon. She passed
Sandy Hook about six hours ago.'

As White paused here, Sargent swung around in
his chair and took another cigar from the box in
the drawer of his desk. ' Have you finished?' he
asked.

' I have finished,' answered White. ' As you
requested, I have told my tale as briefly as possible.
But I have written it out in full, setting down all
the facts in order, and giving dates and figures as
exactly as I could. Perhaps you would like to
glance over it.'

Sargent took the flat little bundle of papers
which White held out to him, and dropped it into

his pocket. He lighted his second cigar from the first. Then he said, pleasantly: 'This is a very pretty little ghost story of yours, Mr. White, but do you think you can get anybody to take any stock in it?'

'I believe the public will take an interest in it —if——'

'If?' asked Sargent, with his cigar in the air.

'If I publish it.'

'Ah, *if* you publish it.' And Sargent smiled meaningly, and the whole expression of his face changed at once. 'Very well. How much?'

'I beg your pardon?' said White, interrogatively.

'How much do you want?'

'Mr. Sargent!' and White rose to his feet, indignantly.

'Sit down again, Mr. White; we are talking business now. How much do you want to suppress this story?'

White clinched the back of the chair firmly in his hand, and said, 'I did not expect to be insulted by the offer of a paltry bribe.'

'Who said anything about a *paltry* bribe? I asked you how much?'

By this time White had recovered his temper. He sat down again. 'You do not know me if you think I am to be bought, Mr. Sargent. I am hesitating as to the publication of the facts in this case because I am not yet quite clear in my own mind as to my duty in the matter.'

'Indeed?' there was a covert sneer in Sargent's manner as he dropped this one word.

'Perhaps self-interest might resolve my doubts,' continued White. 'Perhaps I could more readily make up my mind to say nothing about your connection with the affair of the " Patagonia " if——'

'If——?' repeated Sargent.

'If I felt jealous of your reputation on my own account—in short, if I were a member of your family.'

'You don't want me to adopt you, do you?' asked Sargent, brusquely.

'No, not exactly,' answered White, hesitating, now he had reached the point. 'But I want to marry your daughter.'

Sargent looked at him in silent astonishment. Then he whistled. 'You want to marry my daughter?'

'Yes.'

'Then the main question is not what I think, but what she thinks. Does she want to marry you?'

'She told me so the last time I saw her,' said White, quietly.

Sargent stood up in his surprise. But all he said was, 'What?'

'I asked her to marry me, and she promised to do so—if you would consent.'

'Ah,' said Sargent; 'so you are engaged?'

'Yes,' we are engaged,' answered White.

'But I have always told Dorothy that I would

never consent to her marrying anybody. I want her myself. I do not wish her to leave me.'

'That's what she told me.'

'And yet she has engaged herself to you?'

'We are engaged—yes; but we shall not be married until you give your consent.'

'And you expect me to yield?' asked Sargent, harshly.

'That's why I came to see you to-day,' answered White, gently.

'Well, you are the cheekiest young fellow I ever saw.' And Sargent sat down again, and struck a match to relight his cigar.

White asked anxiously, 'Will you consent?'

Sargent took two or three puffs at his cigar, and replied: 'Of course. I have to consent. That girl makes me do what she pleases. I have never refused her anything yet. If she wants you for a husband, she shall have you.'

'Thank you——' began White.

'You needn't thank me,' interrupted Sargent; 'you had better go and thank her, and tell her you are going to dine with us to-day.'

As Sargent and White came down the stairs of the Bowdoin Building a begging peddler jostled against the speculator, who cursed him cheerfully, and then gave him a quarter. At the foot of the stairs White met Eliphalet Duncan, who was just going up to his office. He felt so happy that he stopped Duncan to tell him he was engaged to

be married, and to ask him if he could guess to
whom.

'Of course,' answered Duncan—'to Miss Sargent.'

Then Sargent and White walked on, and
Duncan went upstairs. As he came to the first
landing he saw a flat little bundle of paper. He
picked it up, and took it into his office for examination, to see if he might discover its owner.

In September, at Newport, toward the end of
the waning season, and just before those who are
always in the thick of gaiety and fashion abandoned Newport for Lenox, there was a wedding. Dorothy Sargent and Robert White were
married.

Sam Sargent, left alone, turned to politics with
his wonted energy. On the evening after his
interview with White in April he had had a bad
quarter of an hour, for he could not find the full
and detailed statement of the 'Patagonia' affair
which White had given, and which he could have
sworn he put in his pocket. For a while he did
not dare give rein to his ambition. If this paper
had fallen into the hands of a political enemy, his
election to any office became impossible. But as
time passed on and he got no news of the missing
document, he began to hope that it had been
destroyed without examination. A few days after
his daughter's wedding he received the nomination
for Congress for which he had intrigued un-

ceasingly, and he had made a pungent little speech accepting the honour.

The next evening the sword of Damocles fell. He received a short, sharp note bidding him find some excuse at once for declining the nomination, or the exact truth would be published concerning his connection with the robbery of the ' Patagonia ' on the First of April. As Sam Sargent read this he knew of a certainty that he had a guardian enemy, and that his political career was at an end for ever. He took up the fatal missive to read it again, and for the first time he noticed that it was written on a type-writer, and that it was signed ' Lafitte.'

'LOVE AT FIRST SIGHT'

A DOUBTFUL day of mingled snow and rain, such as we often have in New York in February, had been followed, as night fell, by a hard frost; and as Robert White mounted the broad brown-stone steps of Mrs. Martin's house and, after ringing the bell, looked across Washington Square to the pseudo-picturesque University building, he felt that form of gratitude toward his hostess which has been defined as a lively sense of benefits to come. His ten-minute walk through the hard slush of the pavements had given an edge to his appetite, and he knew of old that the little dinners of the Duchess of Washington Square were everything that little dinners should be. He anticipated confidently a warm reception by his hospitable hostess; an introduction to a pretty girl, probably as clever as she was good-looking; a dignified procession into the spacious dining-room; a bountiful dinner, neither too long nor too short; as well served as it was well cooked; and at the end a good cup of coffee and a good cigar, and a pleasant quarter of an hour's chat with four or five agreeable men, not the least agreeable of them being Mr. Martin, who

F 2

was known to most people only as Mrs. Martin's husband, but whom White had discovered to be as shrewd and sharp as he was reserved and retiring.

And so it came to pass, except that the state of the streets had made White a little late, wherefore the Duchess was slightly hurried and peremptory. She took him at once under her wing and led him up to a very pretty girl. 'Phyllis,' she said, 'this is Mr. White, to whom I confide you for the evening.'

As White bowed before the young lady whom Mrs. Martin had called Phyllis, he wished that the Duchess had kindly added her patronymic, as it is most embarrassing not to know to whom one is talking. But there was no time for inquiry; the rich velvet curtains which masked the open doorway leading from the parlour into the hall were pushed aside, and the venerable coloured butler announced that dinner was served. White offered his arm to Miss Phyllis, and they filed into the dining-room in the wake of Mr. Martin and Mrs. Sutton; the Duchess, on the arm of Judge Gillespie, brought up the rear.

There were fourteen at table,—a number too large for general conversation, and therefore conducive to confidential talks between any two congenial spirits who might be sitting side by side. White had at his left Mrs. Sutton, but she was a great favourite with Mr. Martin, and White had scarcely a word with her throughout the dinner. On the other side of Miss Phyllis was a thin, short, dyspeptic little man, Mr. C. Mather Hitchcock, whom White knew slightly, and whom Miss Phyllis evidently did not like, as White saw at a glance. So it happened that White and Miss Phyllis were wholly dependent on each other for entertainment as long as they might sit side by side at the Duchess's table.

'A mean day like this makes the comfortable luxury of a house like Mrs. Martin's all the more grateful,' began White, by way of breaking the ice ; 'don't you think so ?'

'It has been a day to make one understand what weather-prophets have in mind when they talk about the average mean temperature of New York,' she answered, smiling.

'I hope you do not wish to insinuate that the average temperature of New York is mean. I have lived here only a few years, but I am prepared to defend the climate of New York to the bitter end.'

'Then you must defend the weather of to-day,' she retorted gaily, 'for it had a very bitter end. I felt like the maid in the garden hanging out the clothes, for down came a black wind to bite off my nose.'

'Just now you remind me rather of the queen in the parlour eating bread and honey.'

'I have an easy retort,' she laughed back. 'I can say you are like the king in his chamber counting out his money : for that is how most New York men seem to spend their days.'

'But I am not a business man,' explained White, thinking that Miss Phyllis was a ready young lady with her wits about her, and regretting again that he had not learnt her name.

'They say that there are only two classes who scorn business and never work—the aristocrats and the tramps,' she rejoined mischievously. 'Am I to infer that you are an aristocrat or a tramp?'

'I regret to say that I am neither the one nor the other. A tramp is often a philosopher—of the peripatetic school of course; and an aristocrat is generally a gentleman, and often a good fellow. No, I am afraid your inference was based on a false premise. I am not a business man, but, all the same, I earn my living by my daily work. I am a journalist, and I am on the staff of the " Gotham Gazette."'

'Oh, you are an editor? I am so glad. I have always wanted to see an editor,' ejaculated Miss Phyllis with increasing interest.

'You may see one now,' he answered. 'I am on exhibition here from seven to nine to-night.'

'And you are really an editor?' she queried, gazing at him curiously.

'I am a journalist and I write brevier, so I suppose I may be considered as a component unit of the editorial plural,' he replied.

'And you write editorials?'

'I do ; I have written yards of them—I might almost say miles of them.'

'How odd! Somehow the editorials of a great

paper always remind me of the edicts of the Council of Ten in Venice—nobody knows whose they are, and yet all men tremble before them.' As she said this, Miss Phyllis looked at him meditatively for a moment, and then she went on, impulsively, 'And what puzzles me is how you ever find anything to say !'

A quiet smile played over White's face as he answered gravely, 'We have to write a good deal, but we do not always say anything in particular.'

'When I read the telegrams,' continued Miss Phyllis, 'especially the political ones, I never know exactly what it's all about until I've read the editorial. Then, of course, it all seems clear enough. But *you* have to make all that up out of your own head. It must be very wearing.'

The young journalist wondered for a second whether this was sarcasm or not ; then he admitted that he had been using up the gray matter of his brain very rapidly of late.

'I know I exhausted myself one election,' she went on, 'when I tried to understand politics. I thought it my duty to hear both sides, so I read two papers. But they contradicted each other so, and they got me so confused, that I had to give it up. Really I hadn't any peace of mind at all until I stopped reading the other paper. Of course I couldn't do without the "Gotham Gazette."'

'Then are all our labours amply rewarded ? ' said White gallantly, thinking that he had only once met a young lady more charming than Miss Phyllis.

'Now tell me, Mr. White, what part of the paper do you write?'

'Tell me what part of the paper you read first —but I think I can guess that. You always begin with the deaths and then pass on to the marriages. Don't you?'

Miss Phyllis hesitated a moment, blushed a little,—whereat White thought her even prettier than he had at first,—and then confessed. 'I do read the deaths first; and why not? Our going out of the world is the most important thing we do in it.'

'Except getting married—and that's why you read the marriages next?' he asked.

'I suppose so. I acknowledge that I read the marriages with delight. Naturally I know very few of the brides, but that is no matter—there is all the more room for pleasant speculation. It's like reading only the last chapter of a novel—you have to invent for yourself all that went before.'

'Then you like the old-fashioned novels, which always ended like the fairy stories, "So they were married and lived happily ever afterward?"' he queried.

'Indeed I do,' she answered vehemently. 'Unless I have orange-blossoms and wedding-cake given to me at the end of a story, I feel cheated.'

'I suppose you insist on a novel's being a love-story?' White inquired.

'If a story isn't a love-story,' she answered energetically, 'it isn't a story at all. Why, when I

was only nine years old, a little chit of a girl, I
wouldn't read Sunday-School books, because there
was no love in them!'

Robert White laughed gently, and said, 'I
spurned the Sunday-school book when I was nine
too, but that was because the bad boys had all the
fun and the good boys had to take all the medicine,
in spite of which, however, they were often cut off
in the flower of their youth.'

'Do you ever write stories, Mr. White?'

'I have been guilty of that evil deed,' he answered. 'I had a tale in the "Gotham Gazette" one
Sunday a few months ago, called "The Parrot that
Talked in his Sleep"; it was a little study in zoö-
logic psychology. Did you read it?'

'I don't seem to recall it,' she hesitated. 'I'm
afraid I must have missed it.'

'Then you missed a great intellectual treat,'
said the journalist, with humorous exaggeration.
'Fiction is stranger than truth sometimes, and there
were absolutely no facts at all in "The Parrot that
Talked in his Sleep."'

'It was a fantastic tale, then?'

'Well, it was rather eccentric.'

'You must send it to me. I like strange, weird
stories—if they do not try to be funny. They say
I haven't any sense of humour, and I certainly do
not like to see anybody trying hard to be funny.'

With a distinct recollection that 'The Parrot
that Talked in his Sleep' had been noticed by
several friendly editors as 'one of the most amusing

and comical conceits ever perpetrated in America,
White thought it best not to promise a copy of it
to Miss Phyllis.

'Perhaps you would prefer another sketch I
published in the "Gotham Gazette,"' he ventured.
'It was called "At the End of his Tether," and it
described a quaint old man who gave up his life to
the collecting of bits of the ropes which had hanged
famous murderers.'

'How gruesome!' she exclaimed, with a little
shudder, although the next minute she asked with
interest: 'And what did he do with them?'

'He arranged them with great care, and labelled
them exactly, and gloated over them until his mind
gave way, and then he spliced them together and
hung himself on a gallows of his own inventing.'

'How delightfully interesting!'

'It was a little sketch after Hawthorne—a long
way after,' he added modestly.

'I just doat on Hawthorne,' remarked Miss
Phyllis critically. 'He never explains things, and
so you have more room for guessing. I do hate
to see everything spelt out plain at the end of a
book. I'm satisfied to know that they got married
and were happy, and I don't care to be told just
how old their children were when they had the
whooping-cough!'

'A hint is as good as a table of statistics to a
sharp reader,' said the journalist. 'I think the
times are ripe for an application to fiction of the
methods Corot used in painting pictures. Father

Corot, as the artists call him, gave us a firm and vigorous conception veiled by a haze of artistic vagueness.'

'That's what I like,' agreed Miss Phyllis. 'I like something left to the imagination.'

'Your approbation encourages me to persevere. I had planned half-a-dozen other unconventional tales, mere trifles, of course, as slight as possible in themselves, but enough with " The Parrot that Talked in his Sleep," and "At the End of his Tether," to make a little book, and I was going to call it " Nightmare's Nests." '

'What an appetising title!' declared the young lady. 'I'm so sorry it is not published now—I couldn't rest till I'd read it.'

'Then I am sure of selling at least one copy.'

'Oh, I should expect you to send me a copy yourself,' said Miss Phyllis archly, 'and to write "with the compliments of the author" on the first page.'

Robert White looked up with a smile, and he caught Miss Phyllis's eye. He noted her bright and animated expression. He thought that only once before had he ever met a prettier or a livelier girl.

'You shall have an early copy,' he said, 'a set of " advance sheets," as the phrase is.'

Here his attention and hers was distracted by the passing of a wonderful preparation of lobster served in sherry, and cooked as though it were terrapin ; this was a speciality of the Duchess's

Virginian cook, and was not to be treated lightly
When this delicacy had been duly considered, Miss
Phyllis turned to him again.

'Can't you tell me one of the stories you are
going to write?' she asked.

'Here—now—at table?'

'Yes; why not?'

'Do you play chess? I mean do you understand the game?'

'I think it is poky; but I have played it with
grandpa.'

'There is a tale I thought of writing, to be
called "The Queen of the Living Chessmen";
but——'

'That's a splendid title. Go on.'

'Are you sure it would interest you?' asked
the author.

'I can't be sure until you begin,' she answered
airily; 'and if it doesn't interest me, I'll change the
subject.'

'And we can talk about the weather.'

'Precisely. And now, do go on!'

She gave an imperious nod, which White could
not but consider charming. There was no lull in
the general conversation around the table. Mr.
Martin was monopolising Mrs. Sutton's attention,
and Mr. C. Mather Hitchcock had at last got into
an animated discussion with the lady on the other
side of him. So White began.

'This, then, is the tale of "The Queen of the
Living Chessmen." Once upon a time——'

' I do like stories which begin with " Once upon a time," ' interrupted Miss Phyllis.

' So far, at least, then, you may like mine. Once upon a time there was a young English surgeon in India. He was a fine, handsome, manly young fellow——'

' Light or dark?' asked the young lady. ' That's a very important question. I don't take half the interest in a hero if he is dark.'

'Then my hero shall be as fair as a young Saxon ought to be. Now, on his way out to India this young fellow heard a great deal about a beautiful English girl, the daughter of a high official in the service of John Company——'

' Is she going to fall in love with him ? ' interrupted Miss Phyllis again.

' She is.'

' Then this is a love-story ?'

'It is indeed,' answered the author, with emphasis.

'Then you may go on,' said the young lady ; ' I think it will interest me.'

And White continued :

' The young doctor had heard so much about her beauty that he was burning with anxiety to behold her. He felt as though the first time he should see her would be an epoch in his life. He was ready to love her at first sight. But when he got to his post he found that she had gone to Calcutta for a long visit, and it might be months before she returned. He possessed his soul in patience, and made friends with her father, and was permitted to inspect a miniature of her, made by the best artist in India. This portrait more than confirmed the tales of her beauty. The sight of her picture produced a strange but powerful effect upon the doctor, and his desire to see the fair original redoubled. From Calcutta came rumours of the havoc she wrought there among the susceptible hearts of the English exiles, but so far as rumour could tell she herself was still heart-free. She had not yet found the man of her choice ; and it was said that she had romantic notions, and would marry only a man who had proved himself worthy, who had, in short, done some deed of daring or determination on her behalf. The young Englishman listened to these rumours with a sinking of the heart, for he had no hope that he could ever do anything to deserve her. At last the news came that she was about to return to her father, and at the same time came an order to the doctor to join an expedition among the hill-tribes. He called on her father before he went, and he got a long look at her miniature, and away he went with a heavy heart for the love he bore a woman he had never seen. No sooner had his party set off than there was trouble with the Hindoos. The British residents and the native princes led a cat-and-dog life, and there began to be great danger of civil war. There were risings in various parts of the country.'

'In what year was this ?'

'I don't know yet,' answered the journalist. 'You see I have only the general idea of the story. I shall have to read up a good deal to get the historical facts and all the little touches of local colour. But I suppose this must have been about a hundred years ago or thereabouts. Will that do?'

'If you don't *know* when your story happened,' said Miss Phyllis, 'of course you can't tell me. But go on, and tell me all you *do* know.'

'Well, the young doctor was captured by a party of natives and taken before a rajah, or whatever they call him, a native prince, who had renounced his semi-allegiance to the British and who had at once revealed his cruelty and rapacity. In fact, the chief into whose hands the young surgeon had fallen was nothing more nor less than a bloodthirsty tyrant. At first he was going to put the doctor to death, but fortunately, just then, one of the lights of the harem fell ill and the doctor cured her. So, instead of being killed, he was made first favourite of the rajah. He had saved his life, although he was no nearer to his liberty.'

'Why, wouldn't the rajah let him go?' asked Miss Phyllis with interest.

'No, he wanted to keep him. He had found it useful to have a physician on the premises, and in future he never meant to be without one. After a few vain appeals, the doctor gave up asking for his liberty. He began to plan an escape without the rajah's leave. One evening the long-sought opportunity arrived, and as a large detachment of English prisoners was brought into town, the doctor slipped out.'

'Did he get away safely?'

'You shall be told in due time. Let us not anticipate, as the story-tellers say. Did I tell you that the rajah had found out that the doctor played chess, and that he had three games with him every night?'

'This is the first I have heard of it,' was the young lady's answer.

'Such was the fact. And this it was which led to the doctor's recapture. On the evening of his escape the rajah wanted his chess a little earlier, and the doctor could not be found; so they scoured the country for him, and brought him before the prince, who bade them load him with chains and cast him into a dungeon cell.'

'And how long did he languish there?'

'Till the next morning only. At high noon he was taken out and the chains were taken off, and he was led into a spacious balcony overlooking a great court-yard. This court-yard was thronged with people and the sides were lined with soldiers. In the centre was a large vacant space. This vacant space was a square composed of many smaller squares of alternating black and white marble. Unconsciously the doctor counted these smaller squares; there were exactly sixty-four — eight in a row and eight rows.'

'Just as though it was a huge chess-board?' inquired Miss Phyllis.

White was flattered by the visible interest this pretty girl took in his narrative.

'It *was* a huge chess-board, nothing else,' he answered, 'and a game of chess was about to be played on it by living chess-men. Soon after the doctor was brought into the gallery, there was a movement in the outskirts of the throng below, and four elephants came in and took their places at the four corners of the gigantic chess-board. Two of these elephants were draped with white and two with black, and their howdahs were shaped like castles. Then came in four horsemen, two on white steeds and two on black, and they took their places next to the castles.'

'They were the knights! Oh, how romantic!' ejaculated the young lady.

'Next came four fools or jesters, for in the Oriental game of chess the bishop is replaced by a clown. Two of these were white men and two were Hindoos. They took their places next to the knights. Then there entered two files of eight soldiers, and the eight white men took the second row on one side while the eight Hindoos faced them on the second row opposite.'

'They were the pawns, I suppose?'

'They were the pawns. The doctor now began to suspect what was going on, and he saw a white man and a Hindoo, both magnificently caparisoned, and with tiny pages supporting the skirts of their

G

robes, enter the square allotted to the kings. Finally in two litters or sedan-chairs the two queens were borne in ; the doctor saw that one was a white woman and the other a Hindoo, but the white pieces were on the side of the court opposite him, and he could not distinguish the features of any of his countrymen—for that they were English captives he felt convinced.'

'But who was to play the game?' asked Miss Phyllis eagerly.

'The rajah and the doctor. The rajah came into the balcony and told the doctor that since he wanted to get away he might have a chance for his life. If he could win the game, the rajah would not only spare his life, but he might depart in peace, and even more, he might select from the English captives any one he chose to depart with him.'

'But if he lost the game?'

'Then he lost his life. For the doctor that game of chess with the living chessmen meant life or death. But the sturdy young Englishman had a stout heart and a strong head, and he was not frightened. Although he had generally managed to lose when playing with the rajah, he knew that he played a finer game. He knew, moreover, that although the rajah was a despot and a bloody-minded villain, yet he would keep his word, and if he lost the game the doctor would be sent away in safety and honour, as had been promised. So the doctor planned his game with

care and played with more skill than the rajah had
suspected him of having. After half a dozen moves
there was an exchange of pawns. The captured
men were led to the sides of the court-yard, and
there stood an executioner, who whipped off their
heads in a second.'

'What!' almost shouted Miss Phyllis. 'Do
you mean to say he killed them?'

'The living chess-men, white or black, English
or Hindoo, were all prisoners and had all been
condemned to death. The rajah was using them
for his amusement before killing them—that was
all. As soon as they were taken in the course of
the game, they were no longer useful, and the
headsman did his work upon them at once.'

'You don't call *this* a love-story, do you?' was
Miss Phyllis's indignant query.

'You shall see. When the doctor saw the fate
of the captured pieces he almost lost his self-control.
But he was a brave man, and in a little while he
regained courage. An attendant explained that
these men would die anyhow, and in time the
doctor got interested in the game and intent on
saving his own life, and he ceased to think about
the lives of the hapless human chess-men. And
the rajah gave him enough to think about. The
rajah, having nothing at stake, and knowing it was
the last game with the doctor, played with unusual
skill and success. With Oriental irony the rajah
had chosen the white pieces, and he kept sending
the white queen on predatory excursions among

G 2

the black chessmen. The doctor saw that if he
did not take the white queen he was a dead man ;
so he laid a trap for her, and the rajah fell into the
trap and sent the white queen close to the black
pieces, taking a black pawn. For the first time the
doctor got a good look at the white queen. His
heart jumped into his mouth and beat so loud that
he thought the rajah must hear it. The white queen
was the beautiful English girl of whom he had
thought so much and so often, and whom he had
never seen. He knew her at a glance, for the miniature was a good likeness, though it could not do
justice to her wonderful beauty ; it was indeed fit
that she should be robed as a queen. As soon as
the doctor saw her he felt that he loved her with the
whole force of his being ; no stroke of love at first
sight was ever more sudden or more irresistible. For
a moment love, astonishment, and fear made him
stand motionless.'

'And what did she do?'

'She could do nothing. And what could he do?
It was a tremendous predicament. If he captured
the white queen, she would be killed at once. If
he did not capture her, the rajah in all probability
would win the game—and then both he and she
would have to die. He had a double incentive to
win the game, to save his own life and to save hers
also, by selecting her as the one to accompany him.
But the game became doubly difficult to win,
because he dare not take the rajah's most powerful
piece. To make the situation more hopeless, the

rajah, seeing that the doctor let him withdraw the queen from a position the full danger of which he discovered as soon as the move was made, and detecting the signals with which the doctor tried to encourage the woman he loved, and to bid her be of good cheer—the rajah began to count on the doctor's unwillingness to take the white queen ; he made rash raids into the doctor's intrenchments and decimated the doctor's slender force. In half an hour the game looked hopeless for the young Englishman. Less than half of the thirty-two living chessmen stood upon the marble squares, and of these barely a third belonged to the doctor. The rajah had the advantage in numbers, in value, and in position.'

'Then how did the doctor get out of it ?'

'The rajah's success overcame his prudence, and he made a first false move. The doctor saw a slight chance, and he studied it out as though it were an ordinary end game or a problem. Suddenly the solution burst upon him. In three swift moves he checkmated the astonished rajah.'

'And saved his own life and hers too?' asked the young lady, with great interest.

'So they were married and lived happily ever afterwards. You see my love story ends as you like them to end.'

'It's all very well,' said Miss Phyllis, 'but the man did everything. I think she ought to have had a chance too.'

It must not be supposed that there had been any break in the continuous courses of Mrs.

Martin's delightful dinner while White was telling
the tale of 'The Queen of the Living Chess-men.'
In fact, he was unable to answer this last remark
of Miss Phyllis's as he was helping himself to a
delicious *mayonnaise* of tomatoes, another speciality
of the Duchess's, who always served it as a self-
respecting *mayonnaise* should be served—in a shal-
low glass dish imbedded in the cracked ice which
filled a deeper dish of silver. So the young lady
had a chance to continue.

'I do not object to the bloodshed and murder
and horrors in your story, of course. I don't mean
that I *like* horrors, as some girls do, but I am not
squeamish about them. What I don't like is your
heroine ; she doesn't *do* anything.'

'She is loved,' answered the author ; 'is not
that sufficient?'

'You *say* she is loved, but how do I know that
she loves back? I have only your word for it; and
you are a man, and so, of course, you may be
mistaken in such matters.'

'What more could I do to convince you of her
affection for her lover?'

'You needn't do anything, but you ought to
have let her do something. I don't know what,
but I feel she ought to have done a deed of some
sort, something grand, heroic, noble,—something
to make my blood run cold with the intensity of
my admiration! I'd like to see her sacrifice her
life for the man she loves.'

'You want a Jeanne d'Arc for a heroine?'

'Rather a Mary Queen of Scots, eager to love and to be loved, and ready to do and to die—a woman with an active spirit, and not a mere passive doll, like the weak girl your doctor married.'

Robert White remarked that her slight excitement had heightened her colour, and that the flush was very becoming to her.

'We shall have to go back,' he said, 'to the days of Rebecca and Rowena, if you insist on having lissome maidens and burly warriors, hurtling arrows and glinting armour, the flash of scarlet and the blare of the trumpet.'

'I don't think so,' she retorted; 'there is heroism in modern life, and in plenty too, though it goes about gravely and in sad-coloured garments. And besides,' she added, changing the subject with feminine readiness, 'you tell us only about the peril they were in, and nothing at all about their love-making. Now, that's the part I like best. I just delight in a good love-scene. I used to wade through Trollope's interminable serials just for the sake of the proposals.'

'It is never too early to mend. I will take your advice, and work up the love interest more. I will show how it was that the young English beauty who was "The Queen of the Living Chessmen" came in time and by slow degrees to confess that the young doctor was the king of her heart.'

'Then I will read it with even more pleasure.'

'But, do you know,' he continued, dropping his mock-heroic intonation, 'that it is not easy to shoot Cupid on the wing? Indeed, it is very difficult to write about love-making.'

'From lack of experience?' inquired Miss Phyllis mischievously.

'Precisely so. Now, how does a man propose?' asked White innocently.

The flush of excitement had faded before this, but suddenly a rich blush mantled her face and neck. For a second she hesitated; then she looked up at White frankly, and said, 'Don't you know?'

Under her direct gaze it was his turn to flush up, and he coloured to the roots of his hair.

'Pray forgive me if I have seemed personal,' he said, 'but I had supposed a young lady's opportunities for observation were so many more than a man's, that I hoped you might be willing to help me.'

'I think that perhaps you are right,' she replied calmly, 'and that "The Queen of the Living Chess-men" will be interesting enough without any love-passages.'

'But I have other stories,' he rejoined eagerly; 'there is one in particular,—it is a love-story, simply a love-story.'

'That will be very nice indeed,' she said seriously, and as though her mind had been recalled suddenly.

'I am going to call it "Love at First Sight." You believe in love at first sight, don't you?'

Again the quick blush crimsoned her face. 'I—I don't quite know,' she answered.

'I thought all young ladies maintained as an article of faith, without which there could be no salvation, that love at first sight was the only genuine love ?'

'I do not know what other girls may think,' said Miss Phyllis, with cold dignity, 'but I have no such foolish ideas !'

White was about to continue the conversation, and to ask her for such hints as she might be able to afford him toward the writing of 'Love at First Sight,' when the Duchess gave the signal for the departure of the ladies. As Miss Phyllis rose White fancied that he caught a faint sigh of relief, and as he lifted back her chair he wondered whether he had been in any way intrusive. She bowed to him as she passed, with the brilliant smile which was, perhaps, her greatest charm. As she left the room his eyes followed her with strange interest. The heavy curtain fell behind the portly back of the Duchess, and the gentlemen were left to their coffee and to their cigars ; but Mat Hitchcock took the chair next to White's, and began at once to talk about himself in his usual effusive manner. The aroma of the coffee and the flavour of his cigar were thus quite spoilt for White, who seized the first opportunity to escape from Hitchcock and to join the ladies. As he entered the spacious parlour Hitchcock captured him again, and although White was able to mitigate the infliction by including two or three other guests in the conversation, it was not until the party began to break up that he

could altogether shake off the incubus.   Then he
saw Miss Phyllis just gliding out of the door, after
having bade the Duchess a fond farewell.

Robert White crossed over to Mrs. Martin at
once. 'I have to thank you for a very delightful
evening,' he began. 'The dinner was a poem,—if
you will excuse the brutality of the compliment,—
and the company were worthy of it—with one
unworthy exception, of course.'

'Oh, Mr. White, you flatter me,' said the pleased
Duchess.

'Indeed, I do not. Very rarely have I heard
such clever talk——'

'Yes,' interrupted Mrs. Martin. 'I do like the
society of intellectual people.'

'And,' continued White, 'I quite lost my heart
to the very pretty girl I took in to dinner.'

'Isn't she charming?' asked Mrs. Martin enthusiastically. 'I think she is the nicest girl in
New York.'

'By the way—do you know, I did not quite
catch her name——'

'Hadn't you ever met before? Why, she is
the daughter of old Judge Van Rensselaer. You
must have heard me talk of Baby Van Rensselaer,
as I always call her? She's engaged to Delancey
Jones, you know. It's just out. She didn't like
him at first, I believe, and she refused him. But
he offered himself again just after we all got back
from Europe this fall, and now she's desperately in
love with him. Dear Jones would have been here

to-night, of course, but he's in Boston building a flat, so I put you in his seat at table. You know Dear Jones, don't you?' And the Duchess paused for a reply.

'Mr. Jones is a cousin of Miss Sargent's, I think——' began White.

'Of Miss Dorothy Sargent? Of course he is. Sam Sargent married his mother's sister. Dorothy's a dear, good girl, isn't she? Do you know her?'

At last White had his chance.

'She is a great friend of mine,' he said, blushing slightly; 'in fact, although it is not yet announced generally, I do not mind telling *you*, Mrs. Martin, that she's engaged to be married.'

'Dorothy Sargent engaged to be married?' cried the Duchess, delighted at a bit of matrimonial news. 'And to whom?'

'To me,' said Robert White.

BRIEF—AS WOMAN'S LOVE

THE imperial will of Napoleon III. decreed, and the ruthless hand of Baron Haussmann traced, a broad street to connect the two great monuments of the histrionic art of France—the Comédie Française and the Opéra—and the resulting Avenue de l'Opéra, not finished until long after the Emperor and the Prefect who planned it had fallen from power for ever, is now a full artery of finance and of fashion. On the right hand side of this thoroughfare, as one walks from the home of French comedy to the temple of French music, and not far from the Rue de la Paix, there is a restaurant called the Café de Paris; and here in a private room, one afternoon early in June, were gathered three Americans, just about to begin their lunch. They had fallen into the French habit of getting through the morning with no other nourishment than a roll and a cup of coffee, so that they were wont to find themselves ready for a more ample mid-day breakfast shortly after twelve. The low ceiling of the *entresol* seemed to make the room in which they sat smaller than it was in reality; but there was ample space for the fourth member of the party, for whom they were then waiting. The melon was on the table, and the *sole à la Mornay*—a speciality of the Café de Paris—had been ordered, but still Dr. Cheever did not come.

Mr. Laurence Laughton crossed over to the window by Mrs. Rudolph Vernon. ' I hope you are not very hungry ?' he said.

' But I am,' she answered ; ' I am famished.'

' So am I,' added her husband.

' Your conduct is unreasonable, and your feelings are reprehensible,' retorted Mr. Laughton. ' As a lady, Mrs. Vernon has no right to an appetite ; and as a poet, Mr. Vernon should scorn the gross joys of the table.'

' The idea !' answered Mrs. Vernon. ' Just as if a woman could live on air ! Why, Uncle Larry, I am hungry enough to eat you.'

Uncle Larry arose quietly, and slyly put the table between himself and the young lady who had thus proclaimed her cannibalistic capacity. But this movement brought him close to her husband, who seized the opportunity.

' I say, Laughton,' he began, ' it is all very well to be a poet, but I am a practical man too, and as a practical man I am simply starving.'

' Well,' said Uncle Larry, ' you will enjoy that *sole à la Mornay* all the more. If it is as good now as it was last year, it is a poem, and it is worthy to be embalmed in verse. I believe that is the phrase they use, isn't it ? '

' And it's a disgusting expression too, I say,'

interposed Mrs. Vernon. 'I don't like to think of Rudolph as an undertaker. It's bad enough to have a doctor for a brother.'

'By the way, my dear,' interrupted her husband, 'are you sure that you told the doctor to meet us here?'

'Of course I am,' she answered. 'He went to the banker's for letters from home while I was putting on my hat to go out, and he sent back a message to say that he had business, and couldn't go to the Salon with us, and I told the messenger to tell him to meet us here to lunch at one o'clock.'

'And it is now nearly half-past,' said Rudolph Vernon, looking at his watch.

'Suppose we don't wait for him?' suggested Mrs. Vernon. 'You know, Rudolph, that if you go without food it upsets you dreadfully.'

'Well,' said Uncle Larry, 'I confess I heard the dumb dinner-bell of hunger some time ago.'

'Dumb dinner-bell of hunger?' repeated the poet, thoughtfully. 'It is a neat figure, but scarcely sufficiently dignified for use—except, perhaps, in comic verse.'

'I should think you would find the pictures in the Salon very valuable to you,' ventured Uncle Larry. 'And it is a pity that the doctor did not get there this morning. Some of the paintings might have been useful to him—as studies in anatomy.'

'They were very indelicate, I thought,' said Mrs. Vernon.

'But I get ideas from them,' continued her poet-husband. 'I took notes for two first-rate sonnets.'

'I saw one picture which suggested a poem to me,' remarked Uncle Larry, with a quiet smile.

'Indeed?' queried Mr. Rudolph Vernon.

'It was one of Henner's, and it was just like all the other Henners I ever saw. It represented a young lady—before the bath. And it seemed to me a perfect illustration of the nursery rhyme:

'Oh, mother, may I go in and swim?'
   'Oh yes, my darling daughter:
Just hang your clothes on a hickory limb,
   And do not go near the water.'

'How absurd!' laughed Mrs. Vernon.

'Well,' said Uncle Larry, 'it may be absurd, but it is singularly exact. Henner's nymphs have always hung their clothes up, but they never are in the water. Now I believe that——'

But Uncle Larry's artistic creed was cut short by the entrance of Dr. Cheever.

'I hope you have not waited for me?' he began, in a deep, grave voice befitting a physician of his wisdom and reputation.

'But we have!' cried his sister. 'Whatever did keep you so long?'

'I was called out unexpectedly,' he answered quietly, 'and the case proved more important than I had supposed.' Something in his manner warned his sister not to press him further with questions.

'Now you *are* here,' said Uncle Larry, 'we
will proceed with our breakfast-at-the-fork, as the
French call it.'

'Do you think melon is wholesome to begin a
meal with?' asked Vernon.

'Why not?' answered the doctor. 'The
French eat it then, and they are not as dyspeptic
as we are.'

'The French don't eat pie!' said Uncle Larry,
laconically. 'We do. In fact, I have sometimes
thought that the typical American might be defined as a travelling interrogation-mark with the
dyspepsia.'

'I wonder,' remarked the doctor, as the waiter
removed the melon and brought in the *sole à la
Mornay*—'I wonder that nobody has ever at-
tempted to explain "Hamlet" by the suggestion
that the young Prince Hamlet has acute chronic
dyspepsia.'

'By the way, Uncle Larry,' asked Mrs. Vernon,
'you never told me how you liked "Hamlet" at
the Opéra last night?'

'Well,' said Uncle Larry, 'a Hamlet who is a
Frenchman and who sings, is to me the abomina-
tion of desolation. But it is such a great play that
even French singing cannot spoil it.'

'The construction of the last act is very feeble,'
remarked the professional poet, critically.

'Very violent, you mean,' suggested his wife.

'In art, violence is feebleness. And the fifth
act of "Hamlet" is the acme of turbulent muddle.'

Uncle Larry and Dr. Cheever exchanged quick glances as Vernon continued :

'I do not deny that it is a great play, a prophetic play even, and deeply philosophical. Indeed, nowhere is the *Weltschmerz* and the *Zeitgeist* more plainly voiced than in " Hamlet " ; but, for all that, the construction of the last act is grossly inartistic.'

'The idea of Ophelia's singing as she floats down the river is absurd,' said Mrs. Vernon, supporting her husband and remembering more accurately the opera of M. Ambroise Thomas than the tragedy of William Shakspere.

'People talk about Shakspere's greatness,' continued Rudolph Vernon, 'and he was great; but look at the chance he had. He came in the nick of time, when men and women had passions, and before all the words were worn out. I'd like to see what Shakspere would do now, when men and women have milk in their veins instead of blood, and when nearly all the fine words in the language are second-hand.'

'You do not believe in a modern Hamlet, then ?' asked Dr. Cheever.

'No ; nor in a modern Ophelia. Women do not go mad and drown themselves nowadays. If they are jilted by Hamlet they marry Guildenstern or Rosencrantz, or, better yet, young Fortinbras.'

'Oh, Rudolph, how can you be so unjust !' was his wife's protest. 'I am sure that women love with as much passion and self-sacrifice as

ever. Why, at Madame Parlier's Institute for
Young Ladies I knew two or three girls quite
capable of loving as Juliet did, and of dying like
Juliet.'

'You are fortunate in your acquaintance,'
answered her husband, 'more fortunate by far than
I, for I do not know any Romeo.'

'Man's love to-day has more common-sense,'
Dr. Cheever suggested.

'Exactly, more common-sense, and therefore
less passion, and a smaller possibility of tragedy.
Shakspere had the inside track, and it is no use for
us modern poets to hope to equal him.'

'I like to think about the fatality of love, and
I hate to hear you say that there are no Romeos
in our time,' said Mrs. Vernon. 'It seems to take
the romance out of life.'

'But there isn't any romance in life any longer,'
rejoined her husband; 'that's my contention. We
have and we can have no Hamlet, no Ophelia, no
Juliet—especially no Romeo.'

Uncle Larry laughed, and suggested:

'You think a modern lover more likely to take
pepsin pills than a deadly poison?'

'I do indeed,' was the poet's answer. Man
now thinks more of his stomach than of his heart,
and where is the poetry in indigestion, I'd like to
know?'

'Well, I don't know,' said Uncle Larry, as the
smile faded from his face. 'I believe in the fatality
of love even in the nineteenth century. I have seen

one man in love with a passion as profound as any Romeo's, and his end was as tragic.'

'Then he was a man born out of time,' urged Rudolph Vernon.

'That may be,' answered Uncle Larry. 'He was a man born to sorrow, and yet he had the happiest nature and the largest heart of any man I ever knew.'

'Is he dead?' asked Mrs. Vernon with a woman's sympathy. 'When did he die?'

'It is nearly two years since I read the sudden news of his death one summer afternoon. It is two years, and yet he has been in my mind all the morning. It may be because I found his last letter to me yesterday in my portfolio, and I had to read it again. So to-day I seem to see his pale handsome face and his bright dark eyes. He had the nobility of soul which makes the true hero of tragedy.'

'But there is no tragedy to-day, as there is no comedy,' argued Rudolph Vernon. 'Instead, we have only *la tragédie bourgeoise* and *la comédie lar-moyante*.'

'I do not think you would say that if you knew his story—the story of his heart and the cause of its breaking,' replied Laurence Laughton. 'To me that is as tragic as anything that ever happened.'

'I do not doubt that,' retorted Vernon, hastily. 'The story of your friend's broken heart may be as tragic as anything that ever *happened*; but in

real life little or nothing happens in the way it
ought to happen artistically.'

'That was Balzac's theory,' said Dr. Cheever,
in his deep voice.

'You remind one of the French painter Boucher,
was it, or Watteau, who complained that nature
put him out,' said Uncle Larry.

'Balzac's or Boucher's, the theory is sound for
all that,' contended the poet. 'In real life we
have only the raw material, and it is crude and
harsh, and it has no beginning and no end—in an
artistic sense, I mean. It is wholly lacking in
symmetry and proportion. And as modern real
life is nearest to us, it is the least artistic and the
most unfinished.'

'Tell him your story, Mr. Laughton, and con-
fute him on the spot,' suggested the doctor.

'Yes, do tell us, Uncle Larry,' said Mrs. Vernon ;
'and then, if it really is tragic, you know, why,
perhaps Rudolph can use it in a poem after all.'

'I'm open to conviction, of course,' admitted
Vernon, 'and I'd like to hear about your friend's
taking off, but I am free to say that I do not
believe it is a rounded and harmonious whole. As
I said, in real life we can get of necessity only
fragments out of a man's life, and a cross section of
a fragment is not art.'

Laurence Laughton hesitated a moment. The
waiter brought in the coffee, and the gentlemen
lighted their cigars.

'It seems almost like sacrilege to the dead to

tell Ralph De Witt's story merely to prove a point,' Laughton began, taking a sharp pull at his tiny cigar. 'But it will free my mind to tell the tale, and it gives me occasion to speak well of him. He was the son of an old friend who had been very kind to me when I was a boy, and I tried to pay to the son the debt of gratitude due to the father. His mother died when he was born, and as an only child his father gave him a double share of love, for himself and for his mother. But when he was only seven years old the battle of Gettysburg was fought, and Lieutenant-Colonel De Witt took command of our regiment after Colonel Delancey Jones had been killed in the first day's fight. As we pressed forward to repel Pickett's charge, De Witt fell from his horse, mortally wounded. He took my hand as I bent over him, and said, "Take care of Ralph." The boy was his last thought, and those were his last words. He had left a will appointing me the boy's guardian, and I do not believe that ever did guardian and ward get on better together than Ralph and I. He was a bright boy, strong, wholesome, manly—a true boy, as he was to be a true man. He worshipped the memory of his father, and in remembrance of his father's death he wanted to be a soldier. At a competitive examination he won his appointment to a cadetship at West Point. He enjoyed his four years of hard work there, and he was graduated first in his

class, going into the Engineers at once as a second
lieutenant. Side by side with his enthusiasm for
the soldier's calling lay a strong interest in science,
and in getting into the Engineers he had accomplished the utmost of his hopes. He had been a
happy boy; he had passed four happy years at
West Point; and he began life with the prospect
of happiness full before him.'

As Laughton paused to light his cigar, which
he had suffered to go out, Mrs. Vernon interjected,
'Why, you said it was to be a tragedy, but it begins
like a comedy. I can almost hear wedding bells
in the distance.'

'Where is the heroine of your tragedy?' asked
Vernon.

'Well,' said Uncle Larry, inhaling a mouthful
of smoke, 'the heroine is at hand.'

'I am glad of that,' remarked Mrs. Vernon,
soaking a lump of sugar in her coffee-spoon. 'I
don't like stories of men only; I want to hear
about a woman.'

'I do not think you will like the woman when
you hear about her,' answered Laughton.

'Why, was she ugly?' asked the lady.

'No; she was almost the most beautiful woman
I ever saw; and I have heard you say that she was
beautiful.'

'Why, Uncle Larry, have I ever seen her?'
inquired Mrs. Vernon, eagerly. 'When was it?
and where?'

'You have seen her, but you do not know her,' answered Laughton.

'Oh, how mysterious! Now go on and tell me all about it, and where your friend met her, and what happened.' And Mrs. Vernon lifted her lump of sugar to her lips and settled back on the divan which ran along one wall of the little room.

'Ralph De Witt got leave of absence in the latter part of the summer of 1881, and he came East for a change. Some friends were going to Mount Desert, and he joined them in a trip to that fascinating summer school of philosophy. His friends went away after a week, but he stayed on. The Duchess of Washington Square—you know Mrs. Martin, of course?' And Laughton paused for an answer.

'Oh dear, yes,' laughed Mrs. Vernon. 'Everybody knows the Duchess.'

'Then you know that she is a born matchmaker?'

'Indeed I do! Why, it was she who introduced Rudolph to me. The dear old soul!' answered Mrs. Vernon.

'Well,' said Uncle Larry, 'then you will not be surprised to be told that she seized on Ralph De Witt as soon as he arrived, and insisted on introducing him to the most beautiful girl in Mount Desert.'

'What was her name?' asked Mrs. Vernon, innocently.

'Her name was Sibylla.'

'Sibylla? That does not help me out. *I* never heard of a Sibylla. Did you?' asked Mrs. Vernon, turning to Dr. Cheever.

'I have met a lady of that name—quite recently,' answered the doctor, and there seemed to be a certain significance in his tone.

'What was she like?' queried the poet.

'I'm not a good hand at an inventory of a woman's charms, but I'll do it as well as I can. She was a blonde with dark eyes. Her face was absolutely perfect in its Greek purity and regularity. Her neck and arms were worthy of the hand of Phidias or Praxiteles; and, magnificent as she seemed, she had a certain marble statuesqueness which makes the allusion even more exact than it is complimentary. In fact, she was not a woman one could compliment on her looks, for her beauty was of so high an order that all praise seemed inadequate and paltry. I heard Mat Hitchcock once say that she walked like a goddess and danced like an angel.'

'And where did this paragon of perfection come from?' asked Mrs. Vernon unenthusiastically.

'From a little town in the interior of New York. Her parents were poor, and they had stinted themselves to send her to a fashionable school in New York. Then she had rich relatives, and it was a wealthy aunt who had taken her to Mount Desert.'

'And your friend Ralph De Witt was the Pygmalion who sought to warm this cold beauty into life?' This was the question of the poet.

'Yes,' answered Uncle Larry; 'he fell in love with her the instant he laid eyes on her, and to him love was no plaything or pastime; it was a passion to endure till death. After three brief weeks of delight in her presence, Ralph had to go back to his post. He left a throng of other admirers around her, and he had had no chance to tell her of his love. To her their slight intimacy was nothing more than a summer flirtation; to him it was a matter of life and death. He returned to his work, thinking that she did not care for him, and he toiled hard to see if he could not forget, or at least forego her. But it was no use. At Christmas he gave it up, and ran over to New York to see her. She was away in the country, but she came back the last day of the year, and he went to wish her a happy New Year. Cupid sometimes pays a New-Year's call, although calling has gone out of fashion in New York; and Ralph De Witt came to me after he left her, with a glow in his face and a look in his eyes which told me he had hope. How handsome he was as he stood in my study, with his back to the fire, telling me the desire of his heart! What a fine, manly fellow he was! Perhaps she had seen this; perhaps she had caught from him the contagion of emotion; perhaps she had really recognised and respected the depth and the nobility of his nature, and the strength of his passion. The next day he saw her again for a few minutes only, but they were enough for him to ask her to be his wife, and for her to accept him as her future husband. They agreed that the engagement should not be announced, for he would not be with her again for months, and as an engaged girl she would not have so good a time.'

'Well!' interrupted Mrs. Vernon, 'she was frank, at all events.'

'She jilted him, I suppose?' asked Rudolph Vernon.

'She married him,' answered Uncle Larry, calmly.

Dr. Cheever looked up with a glance of surprise and said: 'She married him? Sibylla married Ralph? Are you sure?'

'I am quite sure.'

'I did not know that,' replied the doctor, resuming his attitude of silent attention.

'I didn't know you knew anything at all about it,' said the doctor's sister. 'At least you never told me anything.'

Dr. Cheever smiled gravely and said nothing. Uncle Larry continued:

'Early in the spring Ralph De Witt received an appointment he had long wished. He was detailed to take charge of a special survey of the cañons of the Colorado River, a task which would take him several summers, while his winters would be employed in working up the observations made during the warm weather. He wrote to me that the Department would allow him to do this winter work either in Washington or at Newport.'

' I think Newport is just as pleasant in winter as it is in summer,' said Mrs. Vernon.

' Ralph thought so too,' answered Laurence Laughton, 'and he knew that Sibylla was fond of Newport—as she was of everything rich and fashionable. Late in the spring he came to New York. He had ten days to make ready for his long summer in the midst of the marvels of the West. He came here with a fixed idea—to get her to marry him before he went away to his work. You see, he loved her so much that his heart sank at the fear of losing her. He trusted her, but he wanted to make sure. All he wished was to have her bound to him firmly. How he got her consent I cannot imagine, but I suppose the hot fire of his manly love must have thawed her icy heart. He succeeded somehow or other, and the morning of his last day in New York he came to me and told me that she had promised to slip out with him that afternoon to old Dr. Van Zandt's to be married quietly at the rectory. No one was to know of this. It was, in fact, to be only a legal confirmation or ratification of their engagement. The wedding, to which all the world would be invited, was fixed for the following December.'

' And so they were married privately ? ' asked Mrs. Vernon.

' Yes. I was standing on my doorstep, basking in the pleasant sunshine of a beautiful afternoon in May, as Ralph De Witt came up the steps, as radiantly happy as ever man was. "Uncle Larry," said he, as he wrung my hand with a grip of steel, " I have been married nearly half an hour." "Where's the bride?" I asked. "She has gone home to dress for a swell dinner to-night. I've said good-bye to her. I sha'n't see her again for nearly six months. But I do not mind the parting now, for she is mine—mine by the law and the gospel. Uncle Larry, come to Delmonico's and dine with me; I'll treat. Let's have a wedding feast." We had our dinner, and I let him talk about her through the long spring evening, as we walked up and down Fifth Avenue. He poured out his heart to me. There never was a man so happy or so miserable. He had married her, but he had to leave her almost at the steps of the altar. The parting was painful, but he was full of hope and heart, and he trusted her. To hear him talk about her would have made you think that there was only one woman in the whole wide world, and that there never had been her equal. Romeo was not more rhapsodic, nor was Juliet more beautiful than she, though the fair maid of Verona had the advantage of a warm heart, which Sibylla lacked. He told me his dreams and his plans. He had a share in a mine in Colorado, and he was perfecting a new process for reducing ore, a patent for which he expected in a few days. These were in the future. For the present he had his pay and allowances and the income of the little property his mother had left, and these together were enough for them to live on.

He had had an unexpected legacy from an uncle, and of this he had said nothing to Sibylla, for he wished to surprise her with the tiny little cottage he meant to buy her in the outskirts of Newport. There they would live together and be happy in the winter ; while in the summer, while he was away at his field-work, she was to invite her mother and her sister to bear her company. Now I knew her mother, and I knew she had no heart, but only a hard ambition in the place where the heart ought to be. I thought the less Sibylla had to do with her mother, the better for Ralph's chance of happiness. But I said nothing. I never had hinted a doubt of the girl, and, in fact, all my doubts had been killed by the wedding. I never even told him he had better make the best showing he could before her. And I have often wondered whether the end would have been different if he had told her of the house at Newport. But I said nothing ; I let him talk, and he talked of her, and of her only, until at last I lost sight of him as he stood on the platform of the sleeping-car of the Pacific express. I watched the train out of the station, and I have never seen Ralph De Witt again from that day to this—at least, I think not.'

At this last remark, added in a lower tone, Dr. Cheever shot a quick glance of interest at the speaker. He took his cigar from his mouth as though he was about to say something, but apparently he thought better of it, and he returned the cigar to his lips silently.

It was Rudolph Vernon who spoke: 'I can't say that I see anything tragic in your story yet, or even any elements of a possible tragedy. But go on—say your say out. I will reserve criticism until you have told the tale.'

'Yes, go on, Uncle Larry. What happened?' asked Mrs. Vernon.

'For several months nothing happened. I had a letter now and again from Ralph, who was working hard by day and dreaming dreams by night. Private business kept me from spending the summer in Europe. Perhaps it was just as well I was at home, for early in July old Dr. Van Zandt had a stroke and he never left his bed again. When he died, toward the end of August, there was much to be done to get the affairs of the church in order, and most of this work was put on my shoulders as senior warden. I had been down to the Safe Deposit Vaults one hot day, about the first of September, and I bought the first edition of the "Gotham Gazette" to read on my way up-town in the elevated. The first telegram which caught my eye announced the death of Ralph De Witt!'

'Poor fellow!' was Mrs. Vernon's involuntary comment.

'Was it an accident?' asked her brother.

Uncle Larry hesitated a second, and then answered: 'All that the telegram told me was the barren fact of his death. It seems he had insisted on scaling the precipitous side of a cañon; before

1

he had ascended more than a few feet he slipped, and fell head first into the rushing river below, and in a second the current bore him beyond all reach of help.   At first I was stunned by the shock.   I could not believe that the brave boy I had known since he was a baby had had the life dashed out of him by the cruel waters of the Colorado.   Then I suddenly thought of his wife. No one knew of their marriage, or even of their engagement, except me—and I doubted if she were aware of my knowledge.   I knew her very slightly ; I had felt the charm of her beauty, but I had always chilled as she came near me.   I questioned if it were not my duty to break the news to her gently before the cold brutality of a newspaper paragraph told her of her husband's lonely death. The evening paper would not reach her until the next morning, and if I took the three o'clock train I could be in Newport in time to meet her that night.   She was staying at the Sargents', and there was to be a ball that very evening.   I was always very fond of Sam Sargent's daughter Dorothy— Mrs. Bob White, you know—and she had sent me an invitation.   I had accepted, although I had been moved afterward to give up the idea of going. With the " Gotham Gazette " in my hand I made up my mind that it was my duty to go to New-port and to break the news of Ralph De Witt's death as best I could to his unsuspecting wife.'

Laurence Laughton paused in the telling of his tale, and threw his little cigar through the open

window. He leaned over the table and poured out
a tiny glass of brandy. Then he continued :

'Before eleven o'clock that night I was in Newport and at Mr. Sargent's. I asked for Sibylla,
and I was told she was in the ball-room. As
Sargent's house was not large, he had floored over
his lawn, and the ball-room was a tent, hung with
flowers, and lighted by the electric light hidden
behind Japanese umbrellas. As I entered the tent
I thought of Ralph De Witt lying dead and alone,
after a struggle with the angry current of the
Colorado, while his wife, for whom he would have
given his soul, was dancing the German with a
French *attaché*. After many vain attempts I got
speech of her at last. She took my arm, and I
wondered if she could hear the thumping of my
heart. We walked up and down a dim piazza more
fit for the confidences of a lover than for the message
I bore. But if I was excited, she was as calm as
ever. As delicately as I could I broke the fatal
news.'

'How did she take it?' asked Mrs. Vernon.

'She took it coolly. I had thought her cold,
but I confess that her placidity astonished me.
She never lost command over herself. She
showed no feeling whatever. She listened to me
quietly, and said : " Dear me ! what a pity ! Such
a handsome fellow too ! and so promising !
You were old friends, were you not ? It must
be a sad blow to you." This reception fairly
staggered me. Plainly enough she never suspected

that I knew of her engagement and of her marriage. The careless way in which she brushed aside my news and offered her condolence to me was the last thing I had expected. If it was self-control, it was marvellous ; if it was acting there was never better here on the boards of the Comédie Française ; if it was hardness of heart, then it was well for Ralph De Witt that his body lay lifeless on the bank of the Colorado. Just then Sam Sargent came out and joined us. I said nothing, but Sibylla began at once, and told him of Ralph's death. Sargent is a good-hearted fellow, coarse at bottom, it may be, but he can be sympathetic. He knew I loved Ralph, and he asked me for the details of his death with kindness in his voice. She listened, impassive and stately, as I told Sargent the little I knew. I watched her, but she never even changed colour. When I had ended, she said, " I liked Mr. De Witt very much. I used to see a good deal of him at Mount Desert last summer—we went rocking together." Then she took Sargent's arm and went into the house, leaving me speechless. Her indifference was appalling, and I did not know what to think.'

'A very remarkable young woman, I must say,' declared Rudolph Vernon.

'That's just like a man,' said Mrs. Vernon, indignantly. 'Do you suppose she wanted to reveal the secrets of her heart to a stranger? Of course she did not. She kept calm before you and the rest of you men, but when she was alone she dropped the mask of composure and cried all night.'

'I might have given her the benefit of the doubt for a little while, at all events, if——'

'If what?' insisted Mrs. Vernon, with a true woman's instinct of sex defence.

'If I had not met Miss Dorothy Sargent, who came to me in great distress. "Oh, Uncle Larry," she said, "what am I to do? Papa is going to marry again, and he's old enough to be her father too, for she was at school with me, and I was a class ahead of her, and she wasn't clever either. I've no use for a step-mother younger than I am myself, have I? And don't you think he's big enough to know better?" I was in no mood to talk of marrying and of giving in marriage, but I did ask her whom it was her father proposed to marry.'

'It wasn't that Sibylla, was it?' asked Mrs. Vernon.

'It was.'

'But she had refused him?'

'She had accepted him.'

'But she was a married woman!'

'No one knew that. And at any rate she had accepted Sam Sargent. Now you know what manner of man Sam Sargent is. He is a Wall Street speculator, a man of a coarse nature, covered with a layer of refinement, a man of exceeding shrewdness, a man who worshipped success however attained. He's here in Paris now; he was in a box opposite us at the Opéra last

night. Think of a woman's putting aside Ralph
De Witt to take Sam Sargent ! She had found
out that she wanted wealth and the luxury it gives,
and she turned from Ralph to Sargent. She had
no strength of character—worse yet, no heart.
She was as weak as water, and as treacherous.'

'You don't mean to tell me that that woman actually contemplated bigamy ?' demanded
Vernon.

'Well, I don't know what else to call it,'
answered Uncle Larry ; ' but she did not look on it
that way. She thought that her marriage to Ralph
was an idle form, known only to the clergyman
and to themselves. Dr. Van Zandt was dead.
She knew Ralph would not claim her against her
will, and she believed that if she destroyed her
marriage certificate—the only tangible evidence of
her wedding—that she could undo the past and
be a free woman.'

' That's feminine logic with a vengeance,' said
Rudolph Vernon.

'But if the certificate was destroyed why
shouldn't she remarry ?' asked Mrs. Vernon,
innocently.

'When I got back to New York two days
later,' pursued Laughton, 'I found on my desk a
letter from Ralph De Witt. I was reading it over
again last night, after we returned from the Opéra.
I will read it to you, if you like.'

' Yes, do, Uncle Larry,' begged Mrs. Vernon.

Uncle Larry took the letter from his pocket,

and read it as well as he could, for his voice trembled, and more than once he almost broke down.

'In Camp on the Colorado:
'August 30, 1882.

'DEAR UNCLE LARRY,—I got back to the camp last night, after a little *paseo* up in the hills for three weeks, and I found your welcome letter awaiting me. I was pretty tired, for we had been in the saddle thirty-four hours on a stretch, but I read it through before I took off my coat. I had hoped for a letter from Some One Else, but I was disappointed; there must be a breakdown in the mail route somewhere. So I read over again the paragraph in your letter referring to her; and then I tumbled into bed and slept eighteen hours on end. It was nearly noon the next day when I awoke, refreshed and a new man. In truth, I am a new man, improved and made over by the patent process of Cupid and Co. I wake up every morning thanking God for my youth and my strength, and, above all, for the joy of my life. I am as happy as any man ever was. My work is a delight to me, and my future is a dream of bliss. It is no wonder that I build castles in the air; but I remember what Thoreau says, and I am trying to put solid foundations under them. The mine is doing splendidly; it is a boom and not a blizzard this year: and with experience and improved machinery we hope for even better luck next season. And I have finer news yet. You are my

oldest friend, Uncle Larry, and my best friend—
except one, and I know you are not jealous of her
—and so I will tell you first. The patent has been
granted for my new process for reducing ores.
And what is more, a practical man from Leadville,
a regular mining sharp, who saw the working
drawings at my patent agent's, has written to offer
me fifty thousand dollars for a quarter interest.
Fifty thousand dollars! Think of that, old man!
I am a capitalist, a bloated bondholder, and she
shall marry a rich man after all. We'll make a
raid on Tiffany's when I arrive in New York in
the fall, and you shall help me pick out a pair of
solitaires—real solitaires, as the lady said—which
will give her ears a chance to rival her eyes in
their sparkle.

' Good-bye, Uncle Larry, and for ever. When
you read this I shall be dead and out of her
way. What use is life to me if she does not love
me? Her letter has come at last, and I know the
worst. She dreads poverty, she breaks with me,
and I fear she is going to marry another man.
This is a damned bad world, isn't it, Uncle Larry?
But I forgive her ; I cannot help it, for I love her
as much as ever. Poor girl, how she must have suffered before she wrote me that letter ! If she wants
money she shall have it—she shall have all I hoped
to gain. I have no use for it but to make her
happy. There's a man in our party here who was
a lawyer once, and he is drawing up my will for
me. I have made you my executor. You will do

this last favour for me, won't you ?   I leave
everything to her, the little money I have in bank,
my share in the mine, my three-quarters of the
patent--for I have just written to accept the fifty
thousand dollars for the quarter.   I'd like her to
have some money to go on with.   You will attend
to all these things for me ; you have done so much
for me already that I feel I have a right to make
this last request.   This is a long letter, but I want
you to have my last words—my last dying speech
and confession.   Don't think I am going to be
hanged ; a man who is born to be drowned can
never be hanged ; and I am going to be drowned
to-morrow.   I don't know how or when, but a fall
from the rocks is an easy thing to accomplish, and
the river will do the rest.   If she wishes to marry,
I had best take myself out of the way and leave
her free.   After all, what does it matter ? Life is
little or nothing—it is only a prologue, or the posy
of a ring.   It is brief, my lord—as woman's love.
I am in haste to be about my business and to put
an end to it.   The prologue has lasted too long ;
it is time for the real play to begin, the tragedy of
time and eternity, to last until 'the curtain, a
funeral pall, comes down with the rush of a storm.'
Poor Poe was right for once, though I need no
angels to affirm " that the play is the tragedy, Man,
and its hero the conqueror, Worm."   We shall
meet again, Uncle Larry, and until that meeting,
God be with you, and God help me !

                              'RALPH DE WITT.'

'Did she take the legacy?' asked Rudolph Vernon.

'She did indeed,' answered Laughton. 'And Sam Sargent organised a company for working the patent, and floated it in London, and cleared half a million or more out of it. And it was lucky he did, because he got squeezed badly in the Transcontinental Telegraph corner last year, and Ralph De Witt's legacy is all the Sargents have left now.'

'So she actually married Sargent?' was Mrs. Vernon's doleful remark.

'Why not?' asked Laughton, in return. 'Ralph's death left her free to marry whom she pleased.'

'Now you have told your tale, you have proved my assertion,' said Rudolph Vernon. 'In real life the story is incomplete. There is something lacking.'

'She will be punished somehow, never fear,' was Mrs. Vernon's cheerful assertion.

'I think the punishment has begun already,' said Laughton. 'Indeed, it followed fast upon the wrong-doing. At first I fear that Ralph's death was almost a relief to her, for it gave her the freedom she wanted. But no sooner was she married than she began to tremble at her work. With all her money she could not bribe her own thoughts to let her alone. She could not stab her own conscience, and kill it with a single blow. If a conscience must be murdered, it takes a long course of slow poisoning to do it. Then one day there

came a reaction, and she suddenly changed her
mind, and refused to believe that Ralph was dead.
She thinks that he is alive and near her. She
imagines that he watches her, and sends messages
to her by one friend and another. She fancies at
times that he hovers about her, an impalpable
presence. Then, again, he becomes a tangible
entity, a living person, and she declares that she
has seen him standing before her, with his eyes
fixed on her eyes, as though seeking to read the
secret of her soul.'

'That's what the doctor here would call a
curious hallucination,' said Mr. Vernon.

'Well, I don't know,' answered Uncle Larry,
doubtfully.

'Why, the man's *dead*, isn't he?' asked Mrs.
Vernon with interest.

'As I said before,' responded Uncle Larry, 'I
don't know.'

'But what do you think?'

'Well, I don't know what to think,' answered
Mr. Laughton. 'Of course I thought he was dead.
Yet his body was never found, though the sur-
veying party searched for it for ten days or more.
When I heard how Mrs. Sargent felt and what she
fancied, I wondered and I doubted. Now I almost
think I have seen him once, or rather twice.'

'When?'

'Last night.'

'Where?'

'Here—in Paris—at the Opéra. Once as we

entered, and then, again, after the third act. The
first time was in the lobby ; we stood face to face.
If the man who confronted me then was not Ralph
De Witt, he was strangely like him.   I had a
queer, uncanny shiver, but the man looked me in
the eye, and did not know me, and passed on, and
I lost sight of him.'

'And the second time ?' asked Dr. Cheever,
who had hitherto taken no part in the conversation,
although he had listened most attentively.

'As the curtain fell on the third act, I looked
at Mrs. Sargent, who sat by the side of her husband in a box to the right of us.   I saw in her
eyes a look of horror or of fear.   I turned my head,
and there, on the opposite side of the theatre,
stood the same man, Ralph De Witt, or his double.
He was gazing intently at Mrs. Sargent.   I looked
at her again, and I saw her whiten and fall side-
ways.   Her husband caught her in his arms, and
they left the box at once.   When I sought my
dead friend again he was gone.'

There was silence after Laughton stopped
speaking.   Then Rudolph Vernon remarked :
'The romance of real life is better rounded than I
had thought, but it is still incomplete artistically.
There is more behind these facts, and to evolve
this unsubstantial but essential something is the .
duty of the literary artist.'

'Perhaps,' said Dr. Cheever, slowly—'perhaps
a physician may complete the tale as well as an
author.'

'Why, Richard, what do you know about it?' asked his sister.

'Very little indeed, and until this morning I knew even less. If I had heard Mr. Laughton's story yesterday, I could have decided more promptly and more intelligently, it may be, but my decision would have been the same.'

'Were you called in to attend Mrs. Sargent this morning?' asked his sister. 'Oh, why didn't you tell us before?'

'I should not tell you now if the case were not hopeless. I could not go to the Salon with you this morning because I was suddenly summoned to join two French physicians in an examination of Mrs. Sargent's mental condition. There could be no doubt about it, unfortunately; we all agreed; and an hour before I joined you here I signed the order which committed her to an asylum.'

PERCHANCE TO DREAM

I.

MRS. MARTIN, who was known to her lively young friends in New York as the Duchess of Washington Square, had a handsome place on the Hudson, just above West Point. It was called the Eyrie—although, as Dear Jones naturally remarked, that road did not take you there. Every fall, when the banks of the river reddened to their ripest glory, and when the maple had donned its coat of many colours, the Duchess was wont to fill the Eyrie with her young friends. From the Eyrie was heard the report of many an engagement which had hung fire at Newport and at Lenox. The Duchess was fond of having pretty girls about her, and she always invited clever young men to amuse them. She was an admirable hostess, and no one ever regretted that he had accepted her invitation. Mr. Martin, who was, of course, relegated to his proper position as merely the husband of the Duchess, was, in fact, a charming old gentleman, as the clever young men soon discovered when they came to know him. Indeed, although Mrs.

K

Martin was the dominant partner, Mr. Martin was quite as popular as she.

On the afternoon of the last Saturday in October, just as the sudden twilight was closing in on the river, the ferry-boat came gently to its place in the dock of the West Shore Station in Jersey City, and two young men in the thick of the throng which pressed forward to the train were thrust sharply against each other.

'Hello, Charley!' said one of them, recognising his involuntary assailant: 'are you devoting yourself to the popular suburban amusement known as "catching your train"?'

'Hello yourself! I'm not a telephone,' Charley Sutton responded, merrily. 'I'm catching a train to-night because I'm going up to the Eyrie to spend Sunday.'

'So am I,' answered his friend, Mr. Robert White, who was one of the editors of the 'Gotham Gazette,' and who wrote admirably about all aquatic sports under the alluring pen-name of 'Poor Bob White.'

'My wife is up there now,' continued Sutton.

'So is mine,' responded White; 'and Dear Jones and his wife promised to go up on this train.'

By this time the young men were alongside the train: they boarded the Pullman car, and in one of the forward compartments they found Mr. and Mrs. Delancey Jones and also Mrs. Martin.

The Duchess greeted them very cordially.

Come and sit down by me, both of you,' she said, with her pleasant imperiousness : ' I want somebody to talk to me. Dear Jones is getting perfectly horrid. He is so taken up with his wife and the baby now that he isn't half as entertaining as he used to be.'

'Why, Mrs. Martin, how can you say so?' interjected Mrs. Delancey Jones. ' I don't monopolise him at all. I scarcely see anything of him now, he is so busy.'

' You ought not to have introduced us to each other if you didn't want us to fall in love and get married,' said Dear Jones.

' I decline all responsibility on that score,' the Duchess declared. ' People call me a match-maker. Now, I'm nothing of the sort. I never interfere with Providence ; and you know marriages are made in heaven.'

' You believe, then, that all weddings are or-dained by Fate ? ' asked Charley Sutton.

' Indeed I do,' Mrs. Martin answered.

' Well, it *is* a rather comforting doctrine for us happily-married men to believe that our good luck was predestination and not free-will,' said White.

' I wish this predestination was accompanied by a gift of second-sight,' Dear Jones remarked, 'that we might see into the future and know our elective affinity and not be downcast when she rejects us the first time of asking.'

Oh, you men would be too conceited to live if

we didn't take you down now and then,' said his wife, airily.

'Of course *I* knew you didn't mean it,' he went on.

'The idea!' she cried, indignantly.   'I did mean it!   Why, I couldn't bear you then.'

'Still,' White suggested, 'a power to see into the future would simplify courtship, and men would not draw as many blanks in the lottery of matrimony.'

'Second-sight would be a very handy thing to have in the house, anyhow,' Charley Sutton declared. 'A man who had the gift could make a pocketful of rocks in Wall Street.'

'Oh, Delancey,' cried Mrs. Jones, 'wouldn't it be delightful if you could only interpret dreams! You would make your fortune in a month.'

'I'd be sure to predict that the world was coming to an end every time I ate mince-pie,' replied Dear Jones. 'Nobody has had rich visions on prison-fare since Joseph explained his dream to Pharaoh's chief steward.'

'I wonder how the esoteric Buddhists and the psychic-research sharps would explain away that little act of Joseph's,' Charley Sutton remarked, with a fuller admixture than usual of the Californian idiom which he had brought from the home of his boyhood.

'They would call it telepathy, or thought-transference, or mind-reading, or some other of the slang phrases of the adept,' White answered.

'I don't know how much there may be in this Spiritualism,' said the Duchess, in her most impressive manner ; 'but, somehow, I do not feel any right to doubt it altogether. They do very strange things at times, I must say.'

Dear Jones caught Charley Sutton's eye, and they both winked in silent glee at this declaration of principles.

'This play that we have been to see this afternoon,' the Duchess continued—'there is something uncanny about it.'

'The last act is simply thrilling,' added Mrs. Jones : 'I felt as if I must scream out.'

'Where did you go ?' asked White.

'Mrs. Martin and I came in this morning,' Mrs. Jones answered, 'to do some shopping, of course——'

'Of course,' interjected her husband, sarcastically.

'And to go to the matinée at the Manhattan Theatre, to see that English company in the "Bells,"' she continued.

'It is rather an eerie play,' said Sutton. 'The vision in the last act, where Mathias dreams that he has been mesmerised and must answer the accusing questions in spite of himself, is a very strong bit of acting.'

'I can't say I enjoyed it,' Mrs. Martin declared : 'it was too vivid. And I couldn't help thinking how awkward it would be if a man was able to read our thoughts and force us to tell our secrets.'

'If any man had such a power,' said Dear Jones with imperturbable gravity, 'going out into society would be inconveniently risky.'

'It would indeed!' the Duchess declared. Whereupon Dear Jones and Charley Sutton exchanged a wicked wink.

'I'm not given to the interpretation of signs and wonders,' said Dear Jones, 'and I have not paid any special attention to the inexplicable phenomena of occult philosophy——'

'Very good!' interrupted White: '"inexplicable phenomena of occult philosophy" is very good.'

'Really, I don't think you ought to jest on such a serious subject,' said the Duchess, authoritatively.

'I assure you I meant to be very serious indeed,' Mr. Delancey Jones explained: 'I was going on to inform you that once I was told a dream which actually came to pass.'

'You mean the man on the "Barataria"?' asked his wife, eagerly, and with a feminine disregard of strictly grammatical construction.

'Yes.'

'Why, that is just what I was going to ask you to tell Mrs. Martin. I think it is the most wonderful thing I ever heard. Oh, you must tell! It was only a month or so ago, you know, when we were coming back from London. You tell them the rest, Lance: I get too excited when I think about it.'

'Spin us the yarn, as Bob White would say,' remarked Charley Sutton.

'If you can a tale unfold,' White added, 'just freeze the marrow of our bones!'

'It isn't anything to laugh at, I assure you,' cried Mrs. Jones, pathetically. 'You think that because Lance is funny sometimes he can't be serious; but he can! Just wait, and you shall see!'

'Is this a joke?' asked the Duchess, who was always a little uneasy in the presence of a merry jest.

'It is quite serious, Mrs. Martin, I assure you. There are no mystic influences in it, nor any mesmeric nonsense: it is only the story of an extraordinary case of foresight into the future, to which I can bear witness in person, although I have absolutely no explanation to propose.'

'It is a mystery, then?' asked White.

'Precisely,' answered Jones; 'and, with all your detective skill, Bob, I doubt if you can spy out the heart of it.'

The voice of the conductor was heard crying 'All aboard!' a bell rang, a whistle shrieked, and the train glided smoothly out of the station. The little company in the compartment of the Pullman car settled back comfortably to listen to the story Dear Jones was going to tell.

II.

'YOU know,' Mr. Delancey Jones began, 'that I had to go to Paris this summer to get some decorative panels for the parlour of a man whose house I am building. Now, I'm not one of those who think that Paris is short for Paradise, and I wanted to run over and give my order and hurry back. But my wife said she had business in Paris, too——'

'And so I had,' his wife asserted. 'I hadn't a dress fit to be seen in.'

'Consequently,' he continued, disregarding this interruption, ' she went with me ; and she wouldn't go without the baby——'

'I'm not an inhuman wretch, I hope,' declared Mrs. Jones, sharply. 'As if I could leave the child at home! Besides, she needed clothes as much as I did. But there! I won't say another word. When he looks at me like that, I know I've just *got* to hold my tongue for the rest of the day.'

With unruffled placidity Dear Jones continued, 'The man who makes *robes* didn't come to time, the lady who sells *modes* was late, and the conduct of the *lingère* was unconscionable.—I trust,' he asked, turning to his wife, ' that I have applied these technical terms with precision ? '

'Oh yes,' she answered ; 'and you know more about them than most men do.'

'The result was,' Dear Jones went on, ' that we had to give up our passage on the " Provence." By great good luck I managed to get fair state-rooms on the " Barataria," which sailed from Liverpool a fortnight or so later. We had two days in London and a night in Liverpool, and then we went on board the " Barataria," and waked up the next morning in Queenstown, after a night of storm which proved to us that although the ship rolled very little she pitched tremendously. She had a trick of sliding head-first into a wave, and then shivering, and then wagging her tail up and down, in a way which baffles description.'

'You need not attempt to describe it,' said the Duchess, with dignity, raising her handkerchief to her lips.

Dear Jones was magnanimous. 'Well, I won't,' he said. 'I'll leave it to your imagination. We lay off Queenstown all Sunday morning. Early in the afternoon the tender brought us the mails and a few passengers. I leaned over the side of the boat and watched them come up the gangway. One man I couldn't help looking at: there was something very queer about him, and yet I failed to discover what it was. He seemed commonplace enough in manner and in dress; he was of medium size; and at first sight he had no tangible eccentricity. And yet there was an oddity about him, a certain something which seemed to set him apart from the average man. Even now I cannot say exactly wherein this personal peculiarity lay, yet I studied him all the way over, and I found that others had also remarked it. The one thing in which he definitely differed from others was his paleness; he was as white as a ghost with the dyspepsia. He was a man of perhaps fifty; he was clean-shaven; he had very dark hair, so absurdly glossy that I wondered if it were not a wig ; he had sharp black eyes, which were either abnormally restless or else fixed in a preoccupied stare.

'The " Barataria " was crowded, and the ship's company was as mixed as a Broadway car on a Saturday afternoon : there was the regular medley of pilgrims and strangers, republicans and sinners. There was an English official, Sir Kensington Gower, K.C.B., and there was a German antiquary, Herr Julius Feuerwasser, the discoverer of the celebrated Von der Schwindel manuscript. There was a funny little fellow we called the Egyptian, because he was born in Constantinople, of Dutch parents, and had been brought up in China : he had worked in the South African diamond-fields, and he was then a salaried interpreter at a Cuban court. In short, we had on board all sorts and conditions of men, as per passenger-list. We steamed out of Queenstown in the teeth of a stiff gale ; and I shall willingly draw a veil over our feelings for the first two days out. We managed to get on deck and to get into our steamer-chairs and to lie there inert until nightfall ; and that was the utmost we could do. But Wednesday was bright : the wind had died away to a fair breeze, just brisk enough to keep our furnaces at their best ; the waves had gone down ; and so our spirits rose. I went to breakfast late and to lunch early. I found that the odd-looking man I had noted when he came aboard at Queenstown was placed opposite to me, between Herr Julius Feuerwasser and Sir Kensington Gower. They had already become acquainted one with another. During lunch the pale stranger had a fierce discussion with the learned German about the Eleusinian mysteries, and he pushed the Teuton hard, abounding in facts and quotations and revealing himself as a keen master of close logic. Herr Julius lost his temper once as his wary adversary broke through his guard and pinned him with an unfortunate admission; and at dinner we found that the archæologist had applied to the chief steward to change his seat at table. As he was an over-bearing person, I didn't regret his departure.'

'I have seen a German grand duke eat peas with his knife!' said the Duchess, as one who produces a fact of the highest sociological importance.

'Apparently the victor in the debate did not remark the absence of his vanquished foe,' Dear Jones continued, 'for he and the K.C.B. soon got into a most interesting discussion of the Rosicrucians. Obviously enough, Sir Kensington Gower was a learned man, of deep reading and a wide experience of life, and he had given special attention to the subject; but the pale man spoke as one having authority—as though he were the sole surviving repository of the Rosicrucian secret. The talk between him and Sir Kensington was amicable and courteous, and it did not degenerate into a mere duel of words like that in which he had worsted the German. Their conversation was extremely interesting, and I listened intently, having had a chance to slip in a professional allusion when they happened to refer to the connection between Architecture and Masonry. I heard Sir Kensington Gower call the stranger by name—Mr. Blackstone. There seemed to me to be a curious fitness between this name and its wearer : fancifully enough, I saw in the man a certain dignity and a certain prim decision which made the name singularly appropriate. Before dinner was over, the talk turned to lighter topics. As Sir Kensington went below to see after his wife——'

'I remember that *you* didn't come to see after *me !*' interrupted Mrs. Jones, laughing. 'I was left on deck to the tender mercies of the steward. But no matter ; I forgive you.'

Her husband went on with his story, regardless of this feminine personality :

'Mr. Blackstone and I left the table together to get our coffee in the smoking-saloon. Our later conversation had been so easy that I ventured to say to him that a name like his could belong by rights only to a lawyer—or to a coal-dealer. The remark was perhaps impertinent, but it was innocent enough ; yet a sudden flush flitted across his white face, and he gave me a piercing flash from his unfathomable eyes before he answered, shortly, "Yes, I am a lawyer ; and my father owns and works a coal-mine near Newcastle." I did not risk another familiarity. His manner towards me did

not change ; he was as polite and as affable as before :
I studied him in vain to see what might be the
peculiarity I was conscious of but unable to define.
We had our coffee, and, encouraged by my dinner,
I was emboldened to take the cigar Mr. Blackstone
offered me : I have rarely smoked a better. We
sat side by side for a few minutes almost in silence,
watching the smoke of our cigars as it wreathed
upward, forming quaint interrogation-marks in the
air and then fading away 'nt ᵒ nothing. Then the
man we called the Egyptian—I knew him, as he
had crossed with us in the " City of Constantinople " last year—came over and asked us to take
a hand in a little game of poker.'

'He knew the secret wish of your heart, didn't
he ? ' asked Robert White. 'I suggest this as an
appropriate epitaph for Dear Jones's tombstone :
" He played the game." '

'I think I can give you a simpler one,' said the
young Californian,—' just this : " Jones' Bones." '

'I wonder what there is so fascinating to you
men in a game like poker,' the Duchess remarked.
'You all love it. Mr. Martin says that it is the
only game a business-man can afford to play.'

'Mr. Martin is a man of excellent judgment
—as we can see,' said Robert White, bowing
politely.

'Mr. Martin is a man of better manners than to
interrupt me when I am telling a story of the most
recondite psychological interest,' remarked Dear
Jones.

'Don't mind them, Lance,' his wife urged:
'just hurry up to the surprising part of the story,
and they will be glad enough to listen then.'

Thus encouraged, Dear Jones proceeded:

'As I said, the Egyptian came over and asked
us to join in getting up a game. Mr. Blackstone
had been playing with them every afternoon and
evening. We crossed over to an empty table in
the corner where the other players were awaiting
us. There was a change in Blackstone's manner
as he sat down before the cards. I thought I saw
a hotter fire in his eyes. As soon as he took his
seat, he reached out his hand and grasped the
pack which was lying on the table. For the first
time, I noticed how thin and slender and sinewy
his hand was. He gripped the cards like a steel-
trap, holding them for a second or two face down-
ward on the table. Then he cut hastily and looked
at the bottom card. Again the quick flush fled
across his face. He cut again and looked at the
card, and then again. I noted that he had cut a
black court-card three times running. After the
last cut he gripped the pack again, as though he
wished to try a fourth time, but he seemed to
change his mind, for he threw the cards down on
the table and said, "I think I had better not play
to-night." "Why not?" asked the Egyptian.
Blackstone smiled very queerly, and hesitated
again, and then he said, "Because I should win
your money." The Egyptian laughed. "I take
my chance of that," he answered; "you play; you

win—if you can ; I win—if I can." Blackstone smiled again. "You had better not urge me," he replied : "sometimes I can look a little way into the future : I can tell when I am going to be lucky. If I play to-night, I shall win from all of you." The Egyptian laughed again, and then began dealing the cards. "I bet you two shillings," he said to Blackstone, "I get a pot before you." The other players pressed Blackstone to play. Finally he yielded, repeating his warning, "If I play to-night, I shall win everything." Then we began the game.'

'And did he win?' asked Charley Sutton, by his interest confessing his initiation into the freemasonry of poker.

'Well, he did!' Jones answered. 'He emptied my pocket in fifteen minutes. He won on good hands and he won on bad hands. He came in on an ace and got four of a kind. He could fill anything. He could draw a tanyard to a shoestring, —as they say in Kentucky. He had a draught like a chimney on fire. There never was such luck. At last, when he drew a king of spades to make a royal straight flush, the Egyptain surrendered : "I run!" he cried ; "I run like a leetle rabbit!" and he dropped his hands on each side of his head, like the falling ears of a frightened rabbit.'

'Was it a square game?' the young Californian asked, eagerly.

'I do not doubt it,' answered Jones: 'I watched very closely, and I have no reason to think there

was any unfair play. We changed the pack half a
dozen times ; and it made no matter who dealt,
Blackstone held the highest hand.'

'Mr. Blackstone seems to have had a sort of
second-sight for his money,' suggested Robert
White.

'Did his luck continue?' asked Charley Sutton.

'Generally,' Robert White remarked, judicially,
'luck is like milk : no matter how good it is, if you
keep it long enough it is sure to turn.'

'I didn't go into the smoking-saloon the next
day,' Dear Jones explained. 'I——'

'I wouldn't let him!' interrupted Mrs. Jones.
'I thought he had lost enough for one trip : so I
tried to console him by talking over the lovely
things I could have bought in Paris with that
money.'

'But on Friday,' her husband continued, 'as
we left the lunch-table together, Blackstone said to
me, "You did not play yesterday." I told him I
had lost all I could afford. "Yesterday the play
was dull," he said : "it was anybody's game. But
to-day you can have your revenge." I told him I
had had enough for one voyage. "But I insist on
your playing this afternoon," he persisted : "I am
going to lose, and I want you to win your money
back ; I do not want those other men to win from
me what you have lost : it is enough if they get
back what I have gained from them." "But how
do you know that you will lose and that I shall
win?" I asked. He smiled a strange, worn smile,

and answered, " I have my moods, and I can read
them. To-day I shall lose. To-day is Friday,
you know—hangman's day. Friday is always my
unlucky day. I get all my bad news on Friday.
A week ago this morning, for example, I had no
expectation of being where I am to-day." After
saying this, he gave me another of his transfixing
looks, as . though to mark what effect upon me
. this confession might have. Then he urged me
again to take a hand in the game, and at last I
suffered myself to be persuaded. He had pro-
phesied aright, for we all had good luck and he
had bad luck. He played well—brilliantly, even ;
he was not disheartened by his losses ; he held
good cards ; he drew to advantage ; but he was
beaten unceasingly. If he had a good hand, some
one else held a better. If he risked a bluff, he was
called with absolute certainty. In less than an
hour I had won my money back, and I began to
feel ashamed of winning any more. So I was very
glad when my wife sent for me to go on deck. But
just before dinner I looked into the smoking-
saloon for a minute. The five other players sat
around the little table in the corner, exactly as I
had left them three hours before. When the
Egyptian saw me he cried, gleefully, " You made
mistake to go away. We all win, all the time.
We clean him out soon." I looked at Blackstone.
His face was whiter even than before : his eye
caught mine, and I saw in it an expression I could
not define, but it haunted me all night. As I

L

turned to go, he rose and said, " I have had enough for to-day. It is no use to struggle with what is written. Perhaps I may have a more fortunate mood to-morrow." At dinner he sat opposite to me, as usual, but there was no change in his manner. He had lost heavily—far more heavily than he could afford, I fancy—but there was no trace of chagrin about him. He talked as easily and as lightly as before ; and by the time dinner was half over, he and Sir Kensington Gower were deep in a discussion of the tenets of the Theosophists. Sir Kensington was a scoffer, and he mocked at their marvels ; but Blackstone maintained that, however absurd their pretensions were, they had gained at least a glimpse of the truth. He said that there were those alive now who could work wonders more mysterious than any wrought by the witch of Endor. I remember that he told Sir Kensington that the secret archives of Paris recorded certain sharp doings of Cagliostro which passed all explanation.'

'If he knew so much,' asked Charley Sutton, 'why didn't he know enough not to buck against his bad luck ? '

' I can understand that,' Robert White remarked : ' he was like many another man—he did not *believe* what he *knew*.'

' Tell them about the dream, Lance,' said Mrs. Jones.

' I'm coming to that now,' answered her husband. ' I have not yet told you that, in spite of our bad weather the first two days out, we had made a splendid run—almost the best on record. By Friday evening it was evident that, unless there were an accident of some sort, we should get inside of Sandy Hook some time on Saturday night—probably a little before midnight. So on Saturday morning we all got up with a sense of relief at our early delivery from our floating gaol. You have heard of the saying that going to sea is as bad as going to prison, with the added chance of drowning?'

'I have heard the saying,' answered Bob White, indignantly—for he was always quick to praise a seafaring life—'and I think that the man who said it was not born to be drowned.'

'I believe you are web-footed,' returned Dear Jones: 'most of us are not; and we were delighted to get within hail of the coast. It was a lovely day, and the sea was as smooth as I ever saw it. We made a run of four hundred and sixty-eight miles at noon; we took our pilot one hour later; we sent up our rocket and burned our Roman candles off Fire Island about nine that evening; and we ran inside Sandy Hook a little after eleven. Shortly before we had crossed the bar, and as the lights of the coast were beginning to get more and more distinct, Mr. Blackstone joined me, while I was standing near the captain's room. The light from the electric lamps on the stairs fell on his head, and I marked the same uncanny smile which had played about his face when he rose from the

card-table after losing his money the day before.
We walked the length of the ship two or three
times, exchanging commonplaces about America.
I found that he had never been out of England
before ; but he had improved his time on the boat,
for he had already. mastered the topography of
Manhattan Island and of New York Bay. He
asked me how close we should come to the shore
when we entered the Hook, and whether we should
anchor at Quarantine in mid-stream or alongside a
dock. When I had answered his questions as best I
could, he was silent for a little space. Then, suddenly, as we came to the end of the ship, he stopped,
and asked me if I were superstitious. I laughed,
and answered that I was like the man who did
not believe in ghosts but was afraid of them. "I
thought so," he returned. "I thought you were
not one of the narrow and self-satisfied souls who
believe only what they can prove, and who cannot
imagine circumstances under which two and two
may not make four. Now, I am superstitious—
if a belief in omens, dreams, and other manifesta-
tions of the unseen can fairly be called a super-
stition. I cannot help lending credence to these
things, for every event of my life has taught me to
rely on the warnings and the promises I receive
from the unknown. I do not always understand
the message ; but if I disobey it when I do com-
prehend, I am sorely punished. I had a dream
last night which I cannot interpret. Perhaps you
may help me." I confess that I was impressed

by his earnestness; and, not without a share of
curiosity, I told him I should be glad to listen. He
transfixed me with another rapid glance, and then
he said, " This was my dream. I dreamed that it
was to-morrow morning,—Sunday morning,—and
that I was in New York. I was reading a newspaper: there is a paper in New York called the
'Gotham Gazette'?" I told him that there was
such a journal. " Is it published on Sunday?" he
asked. I explained that it sold more copies on
Sunday than on any other day of the week.'

'One hundred and thirty-seven thousand last
Sunday,' interrupted Robert White, smiling, ' according to the sworn statement of the foreman of
the press-room: advertisers will do well, et cetera,
et cetera.'

'For particulars, see small bills,' added Charley
Sutton.

Dear Jones paid no attention to these unnecessary remarks.

'Blackstone repeated,' he continued, 'that he
dreamt he was in New York on Sunday morning
reading the " Gotham Gazette ; " and he told me he
had been trying all day to remember exactly what
it was he had read in it, but his recollections were
vague, and he could recall with precision only four
passages from the paper. " You know," he said to
me,"how old and solid the house of Blough Brothers
and Company is?" I answered that I knew that
they were as safe a bank as could be found in
Lombard Street. " The first thing I read in the

'Gotham Gazette' of to-morrow," he said, " was a message from London announcing that Blough Brothers and Company had failed the day before— that is, to-day, Saturday." I laughed easily, and told him that he ought not to give a second thought to a dream as wild as his, for I supposed that Blough Brothers and Company were as safe as the Bank of England. He shot another sharp glance through me, and answered, after a second's hesitation, that stranger things had happened than the failure of Blough Brothers and Company. Then he went on to tell me the second of the things he was able to recall from his vague memory of the " Gotham Gazette " of Sunday morning. You remember the great steam-yacht race—the international match between Joshua Hoffman's " Rhadamanthus " and the English boat the " Skyrocket "? Well, that race was to come off that very Saturday: it had been decided probably only five or six hours before our talk. Blackstone told me that he had read a full account of it in the " Gotham Gazette " of the next day, and that it had been an even race, but that from the start the American yacht had led a little, and that the English boat had been beaten by less than ten minutes. The third thing he had read in the paper was a review of a book. " I think I have heard you refer to Mr. Rudolph Vernon, the poet, as a friend of yours ? " he asked. I said I knew Vernon, and that I expected to read his new poem as soon as it was published. "It is called ' An Epic of Ghosts,' and there was a long criticism of it in the ' Gotham Gazette,' " said Blackstone—-" a criticism which began by calling it one of the most peculiar of poems and by declaring that its effect on the reader was ghastly rather than ghostly." '

' And he told you this the night before you arrived?' asked Robert White, very much interested. ' Why——'

' Let me tell my tale,' answered Dear Jones : ' you can cross-question me afterwards. I shall not be long now.'

' And what was the fourth item he remembered ?' the Duchess inquired.

' The fourth item,' Dear Jones responded, ' was a paragraph announcing the arrival in New York of the steamship " Barataria "—the boat in the stern of which we were then standing—and noting that one of the passengers was mysteriously missing, having apparently committed suicide by jumping overboard the night before. With involuntary haste I asked him the name of this passenger. " It was not given in the newspaper," he answered, " or, if it was, I cannot recall it." We stood for a moment silently side by side, gazing at the phosphorescent wake of the ship. The second officer, Mr. Macdonough, came aft just then, and I walked back with him to return a book I had borrowed. I found my wife had gone to bed ; and in a few minutes I was asleep, having given little heed to Blackstone's dream, vividly as he had recited its unusual circumstances. The next morning we

were busied with the wearying preliminaries of dis-
embarking, and I did not notice the absence of
Blackstone from the breakfast table. When we
had been warped into dock and had signed our
papers before the custom-house officials, we left the
boat and went down on the wharf to wait for our
trunks, seven of which were at the very bottom of
the hold. A newsboy offered me the Sunday
papers, and I bought the " Gotham Gazette." The
first words that met my eye were the headlines of
a cable message : " Heavy Failure in London—
Sudden Stoppage of Blough Brothers and Company." The next thing I saw was an account of
the great steam-yacht race. As you know, the
" Rhadamanthus " had beaten the " Skyrocket " by
eight minutes. I could not but recall Blackstone's
dream, and I instantly tore the newspaper open,
that I might see if there were a review of Rudolph
Vernon's "Epic of Ghosts;" and there it was.
The criticism began by calling it the most peculiar
of poems and by saying that its effect was ghastly
rather than ghostly. Then I searched for the
fourth item of the dream. But I could not find it.
That one alone of the four things he had told me
was not in the paper. There was nothing about
the " Barataria " but the formal announcement of
our arrival in the column of shipping news. Although the fourth item was not to be found, the
presence of the other three was startling enough,
it seemed to me, and I thought that Blackstone
would be interested to see the real "Gotham

Gazette " of Sunday morning, that he might compare it with the " Gotham Gazette " he had read in his dream. I looked about on the dock, but he was not visible. I went back on the boat, but I could not lay eyes on him. I asked our table-steward and others, but no one had seen him. At last I went to Mr. Macdonough, the second officer, to inquire his whereabouts. Before I had more than mentioned Blackstone's name, Mr. Macdonough became very serious. " I cannot tell you where Mr. Blackstone is, for I do not know," he said : " in fact, nobody knows. He is missing. It is quite a mystery what has become of him. He has not been seen since we left him last night — you and I. So far as I can judge, we were the last to speak to him or to see him. All trace of him is lost since we walked forward last night, leaving him standing in the stern of the ship. He did not sleep in his state-room, so his steward says. We do not wish to think that he has jumped overboard, but I must confess it looks like it. Did he ever say anything to you which makes you think he might commit suicide? " I answered that I could recall nothing pointing towards self-destruction. " He was a queer man," said Mr. Macdonough, " a very queer man, and I fear we shall never see him again." And, so far as I know, nobody has ever seen him again.'

As Dear Jones came to the end of his story, the rattling train plunged into a long tunnel.

III.

WHEN the train at last shook itself out of the tunnel, Robert White was the first to break the silence.

'To sum up,' he said to Dear Jones, 'this man who called himself Blackstone told you on Saturday evening four things which he had dreamt would be in the "Gotham Gazette" of Sunday morning. Three of these things were in the "Gotham Gazette" and, while the fourth item was absent from the newspaper, the suicide it recorded had apparently taken place?'

'Yes,' answered Dear Jones.

'How do you account for this extraordinary manifestation of the power of second-sight operating during sleep?' White asked.

Dear Jones replied, shortly:

'Oh, I do not account for it.'

'What have you to suggest?' White inquired.

'I haven't anything to suggest,' Dear Jones answered. 'I have given you the facts as I know them   Every man is free to interpret them to please himself.   I tell the tale only: I have not hinted at any explanation, either natural or supernatural.'

'Perhaps Mr. White can unravel the mystery,' said Mrs. Jones, with just a tinge of acerbity in her manner.

'No,' White returned, thus attacked in the

flank—'no, I have no explanation to offer—at least, not until I have fuller information.'

'I have emptied myself of the facts in the case,' retorted Dear Jones, 'and a cider-press couldn't get any more details out of me.'

With an amiable desire to pour oil on waters which might be troubled, the Duchess remarked, pleasantly, 'I think Dear Jones has told us a most interesting story, and I'm sure we ought to be obliged to him.'

Dear Jones arose and bowed his thanks. Just then the train went sharply around a curve, and Dear Jones resumed his seat in the car with awkward promptness. As he sat down, Robert White looked up at him musingly. At length he spoke :

'You say the man called himself Blackstone ?'

'Yes.'

'He was a peculiar-looking man, you say,' Robert White continued, 'and yet you could not declare wherein his oddity lay. He was of medium size, a little under the average height, and a little inclined to be stout. He was about fifty years old. He wore a black wig. He had a very white face. His dark eyes were restless when they were not fixed in a vague stare——'

'Why,' cried Dear Jones, 'how did you know that ?'

'He had a long, full beard,' Robert White went on ; when Dear Jones broke in again :

'Oh, no : he was clean-shaven.'

'Ah !' said Robert White, 'perhaps he had

removed his beard to change his appearance. Did he have the blue chin one sees in a man whose face is naturally hairy?'

'He had,' answered Dear Jones; 'and the deadly pallor of his cheeks made this azure of his jaw more obvious.'

'I am inclined to think,' Robert White said, slowly—'I am inclined to think that the man who told you his alleged dream, and who called himself Blackstone, was John Coke, the chief clerk and confidential manager of Blough Brothers and Company ——'

'The firm that failed?' the Duchess asked.

'Precisely,' was the answer; 'and he was the cause of the failure—he and Braxton Blough, a younger son of the senior partner. They both absconded on the Saturday before the failure—the Saturday you sailed : Coke could easily have left London with the mail and joined you at Queenstown. I took a great interest in the case, for my father-in-law lost a lot of money he had sent over to be used in operating in the London Stock Exchange.'

'I shouldn't wonder if you were right in your supposition, Bob,' said Charley Sutton; 'and of course if the man had cleaned out Blough Brothers and Company he could make a pretty close guess when they were likely to suspend. Besides, Blackstone is just the sort of slantindicular name a man called Coke would take.'

'Coke?' repeated the Duchess; 'Coke? Isn't

that the name of the Englishman Mr. Hitchcock used to talk to us about in London?'

'Yes,' answered Mrs. Jones; 'I think I have heard Mr. Hitchcock speak of a Mr. Coke.'

'White looked up quickly with a smile. 'Do you mean Mat Hitchcock?'

'Mr. C. Mather Hitchcock is the gentleman I mean,' replied Mrs. Martin.

'Ah!' said White significantly.

'I saw a good deal of him last summer in London, and I heard him speak of a Mr. Coke several times. I think he said he was the manager or director or something of Blough Brothers and Company. I know he told me that Mr. Coke was the best judge of sherry and of poetry in all England. I own I thought the conjunction rather odd.'

'Mrs. Martin,' said Robert White, 'you have given us the explanation of another of the predictions in the alleged Mr. Blackstone's alleged dream. I happen to know that, owing to a set of curious circumstances, little Mat Hitchcock wrote the review of the " Epic of Ghosts" which appeared in the "Gotham Gazette."'

'And you think he showed what he had written to Coke before he sent it off to the paper?' asked Dear Jones.

'Isn't it just like him?' White returned.

Dear Jones smiled, and answered that Mat Hitchcock was both leaky and conceited, and that he probably did show his review to everybody within range.

'But how did this Mr. Blackstone know that the review would appear on that particular Sunday morning?' asked Mrs. Jones, with a slightly aggressive scepticism.

'He didn't *know* it,' answered White; 'he just guessed it; and it was not so very remarkable a guess either, if he knew when the review was posted in London, as the "Gotham Gazette" prints book-notices only on Sundays.'

'Still, it was a most extraordinary dream,' said the Duchess, with dignity, not altogether approving of any attempt to explain away anything purporting to be supernatural.

'The failure of Blough Brothers and Company was remarkable, if you like,' Robert White continued. 'The house was more than a century old; it held the highest position in Lombard Street; it was supposed to be conservative and safe; and yet for the past five years it had been little better than an empty shell. This man Coke was allowed to do pretty much as he pleased; and he and Braxton Blough, the younger son of old Sir Barwood Blough, the head of the house, were as thick as thieves—I use the phrase advisedly.'

'Thank you,' said Mrs. Jones, with a chilly smile.

'They speculated in stocks,' Robert White pursued; 'they loaded themselves up with cats and dogs; they took little fliers in such inflammable material as Turkish and Egyptian bonds; and they went on the turf together. They owned

race-horses together as " Mr. Littleton ; " and that's
another bit of evidence that your Mr. Blackstone
was really this man Coke. You see? Coke—
Littleton—Blackstone?'

'I see,' answered Dear Jones.

'When the game was up, there was a warrant
out for Coke, but he had been gone for a week.
It was supposed he had run over to Paris ; but
that must have been a mere blind of his, since
he came over here on the " Barataria " with you.'

'He came over with me,' said Dear Jones,
quietly, ' but he did not land with me.'

'Poor Braxton Blough had been led astray by
Coke, who tempted him and got him in his power
and kept him under his thumb. When the bubble
burst he disappeared too, and it is supposed that
he took the Queen's shilling and is now a private
at the Cape of Good Hope. He wasn't in England
when poor old Sir Barwood Blough died of a
broken heart. Braxton had always been his favourite son, and he had spared the rod and spoiled
the child.'

'Braxton Blough?' repeated the Duchess.
'Surely I have met a man of that name ; and I
think it was at the dinner Lord Shandygaff gave
us at Greenwich.'

'I remember him now,' broke in Dear Jones—
'a dark, gipsy-looking fellow. I know I remarked
on the difference between him and Lord Shandygaff, who was the very type of an Irish sportsman,
with all that the word implies.'

Robert White whistled.

'Oh, I beg your pardon,' he cried, hastily, as Mrs. Martin looked at him with surprise. 'You will forgive me when I explain. Now we have stumbled on something really extraordinary. You know those odd little Japanese puzzles—just a lot of curiously-shaped bits which you can fit together into a perfect square ?'

'I have known them from my youth up,' answered Dear Jones, dryly ; 'and I see nothing extraordinary in them.'

'I refer to them only as an illustration,' Robert White returned. 'You tell us a tale of a dream and its fulfilment ; you set forth a puzzle, but there are several little bits wanting ; the square is not perfect ; there is a hole in the centre. Now, as it happens, we here who have heard the tale can complete the square. We can fill the hole in the centre, for we chance to have concealed about our persons the little bits which were missing. And Mrs. Martin has just produced one of them. You met Mr. Braxton Blough at a dinner given by Lord Shandygaff ; and it was natural that you should, for the two men had many tastes in common, and I have heard that they were very intimate. Indeed, next to Coke, Lord Shandygaff was Braxton Blough's closest friend. And this provides us with a possible explanation of another of the alleged predictions in the alleged dream of the alleged Blackstone.'

'How so ?' asked Charley Sutton.

' I confess I don't see it,' said Dear Jones.

' That's because you do not know the secret history of the steam-yacht race,' Robert White answered. ' Lord Shandygaff is the owner of the " Skyrocket " ; he is a betting man ; he was in New York for a fortnight before the race came off ; and yet he did not back his boat as though he believed she would win. Now, I have been told, and I believe, that when the match had been made and the money put up, a rumour of the speed made by the " Rhadamanthus " in a private trial over a measured mile, after Joshua Hoffman had put in those new boilers, reached the ears of the owner of the " Skyrocket." It is said that Lord Shandygaff then had a private trial of his yacht over a measured mile under similar conditions of wind and weather as that of the " Rhadamanthus," and he discovered, to his disappointment and disgust, that his boat was going to be beaten. I have understood that he came to the conclusion, then and there, that he was going to lose the race and his twenty-five thousand dollars—unless there should be a stiff gale of wind when the match came off, in which case he thought he might have a fair chance of winning.'

' Well ? ' asked Charley Sutton, as Robert White paused.

' Well,' said White, ' if what I have stated on information and belief is true, if Lord Shandygaff believed that his boat would be beaten, his intimate friend Braxton Blough would not be kept in the dark ; and whatever light Braxton Blough might have he would share with his intimate friend Coke. Therefore your friend the alleged Blackstone, when he told you his alleged dream on Saturday, the day of the race, knew that there was smooth water and a light breeze only, and that therefore the " Rhadamanthus " had probably beaten the " Skyrocket " from start to finish.'

' I see,' said Charley Sutton, meditatively.

Mrs. Jones looked at Mr. White with not a little dissatisfaction, saying—

' You have tried very hard to explain away this Mr. Blackstone's dream as far as the failure of Blough Brothers and Company is concerned, and the review of Mr. Vernon's book, and the race between the " Rhadamanthus"and the " Skyrocket " ; but how do you account for the suicide ? '

' How do you know there was any suicide ? ' asked Robert White, with a slight smile.

' It was in the " Gotham Gazette "—your own paper,' she said, with ill-concealed triumph.

' It was in the " Gotham Gazette " which Coke said he had seen in a vision,' White returned ; ' but I do not think it was ever in any " Gotham Gazette " sent out from our office in Park Row.'

' But I thought——' began Mrs. Jones, when her husband interrupted.

' I'm afraid it is no use arguing with White,' he

said : 'he seems to have all the facts at his fingers' ends.'

'Thank you,' White rejoined. 'I wish I had my fingers' ends on Coke's collar.'

'That's just what I wanted to ask you,' said Dear Jones. 'Where is he ?'

'How do I know ?' returned White.

'What do you think ?' Dear Jones asked.

'I don't know what to think,' answered Robert White ; 'the facts fail me. Probably the "Barataria" was not very far from shore when she anchored off Quarantine that night, soon after you and Mr. Macdonough left him in the stern of the ship ?'

'We were within pistol-shot of the health officer's dock, I suppose,' replied Dear Jones.

'Then,' said Robert White, 'perhaps Coke jumped overboard and swam ashore, and so killed the trail by taking water. We have an extradition treaty with Great Britain, and he may have told you his dream so that you could bear witness in case he was tracked by the detectives. Perhaps, however, he told you the truth when he told you his dream.'

'I shall always believe that,' Mrs. Jones remarked.

'So shall I,' said Mrs. Martin. 'It is very unpleasant to destroy one's faith in anything. It is so much better to believe all one can : at least that is my opinion.'

This opinion was handed down by the Duchess with an air which implied that no appeal could be taken.

Robert White wisely held his peace.

Then the train slackened before stopping at the station where Mrs. Martin's carriage was awaiting them.

PERTURBED SPIRITS

I.

WHEN it was announced that Mr. Francis Meredith had been appointed secretary to the council
of the Saint Nicholas Relief Society, the friends of
the other candidates for that office were violently
indignant, and declared that the appointment was
one conspicuously unfit to be made. The friends
of Mr. Francis Meredith smiled pleasantly as they
protested mildly in his behalf ; they said that he
would do very well after he mastered the duties of
the post, and that the work was not onerous, even
for a man wholly unused to any regular occupa-
tion ; but while they were saying with their tongues
that Fanny Meredith was a good fellow, in
their hearts they were wondering how a round
young man would manage in a square hole. From
this it may be inferred that the opponents of the
appointment were altogether in the right, and that
one fortunate man owed the place to a freak of
favouritism.

It may serve to indicate the character of Mr.
Francis Meredith to record that to his intimates he
was known, not as Frank, but as Fanny. He was

a charming and most ladylike young man, who
toiled not neither did he spin. He owed his ex-
emption from labour and his social standing to the
fact that he was the only son of his mother, and
she a widow of large wealth. He had managed,
somehow or other, to creep through college in the
course of five years. He was a kindly youth, but
heedless, careless, scatterbrained, and fixing his
mind with ease only on the one object of his existence—the conducting of a cotillion. To conduct
the cotillion decently and in order seemed to
Fanny Meredith to be the crowning glory of a young
gentleman's career. Unfortunately his mother's
trustee made unwise investments and died, leaving
his affairs curiously entangled, and it became necessary for Meredith to do something for himself.
He scorned a place under Government ; besides, he
could not pass the examination with any hope of
appointment. As it happened, Mrs. Meredith's
trustee had been the secretary of the council of the
Saint Nicholas Relief Society, and his death made
it possible to work out a sort of poetic justice by
giving the post to Fanny Meredith.

It is difficult to speak without awe of that
august conclave, the council of the Saint Nicholas
Relief Society. During the original Dutch ownership of Manhattan Island, and before New Amsterdam experienced a change of heart and became
New York, certain worthy burghers of the city had
combined in a benevolent association which continued its labours even after the English capture of

the colony and through the long struggle of the Revolution. When at last New York was firmly established as the Empire City, no one of its institutions was more deeply rooted or more abundantly flourishing than the Saint Nicholas Relief Society. It was rich, for it had received lands and tenements and hereditaments which had multiplied in value and increased in income with the growth of the city. It did much good. It was admirably managed. It had a delightful aroma of antiquity, denied to most American institutions. It was fashionable. It was exclusive. To be a member of the Saint Nicholas Relief Society was the New York equivalent to the New England ownership of a portrait by Copley—it was a certificate of gentle birth. To be elected to the council of the Saint Nicholas Relief Society was indisputable evidence that a man's family had been held in honour here in New York for two centuries. Just as the court circles of Austria are closed to any one who cannot show sixteen quarterings, so the unwritten law of the Saint Nicholas Relief Society forbade the election to the council of any one whose ancestors had not settled in Manhattan Island before it surrendered to Colonel Nicolls in 1664.

Among the descendants of the scant fifteen hundred inhabitants of New Amsterdam were not a few shrewd men of business. The affairs of the Saint Nicholas Relief Society were always ably and adroitly managed, and the property of the

society was well administered. Its annual revenues
were greatly increased by a yearly ball given just
before Lent allowed the ladies of fashion time to
repent of their sins.   This public ball—for it was
public practically, as any man might enter who
could pay the high price asked for a ticket—being
patronised by the most fashionable ladies of New
York, was always crushingly attended, to the re-
plenishment of the coffers of the charity.   To this
public ball there succeeded, after the interval of
Lent, a private dinner of the council, invariably
given on the Tuesday in Easter week, the Tuesday
after. Paas.   The Dutch word still lingers, and perhaps the Paas dinner of the council of the Saint
Nicholas Relief Society may have helped to keep it
alive and in the mouths of men.

To attend to the annual ball and to the Paas
dinner were the chief duties of the secretary of the
council ; it is possible even to assert that these
were his sole duties.   He had nothing whatever to
do with the management of the society ; he was
the secretary of the council only ; and it was precisely because the obligations of the office were
little more than ornamental that the friends of Mr.
Francis Meredith maintained his perfect ability to
fulfil them satisfactorily.   He had been elected at
the January meeting of the council, and he was
told to exercise a general supervision over the
arrangements of the ball, which was to take place
just in the middle of February—on Saint Valentine's Day, in fact.

' I wonder how Fanny Meredith will make out,' said Mr. Delancey Jones, when he heard of the appointment. ' Fanny Meredith is a good-looking fellow, and a good fellow too, and the girls all say he dances divinely ; but he is more different kinds of a fool than any other man I know ! '

As it happened, Fanny Meredith had very little to do with the ball, but he did that little wrong. He blundered in every inconceivable manner and with the most imperturbable good humour. He altered the advertisements, for one thing, just as they were going to the newspapers and without consultation with any one ; and the next morning the members of the council were shocked to see that tickets would be for sale at the door until midnight—there having been hitherto a pleasing convention that tickets could be had only by those vouched for by members of the society. Then, at the February meeting of the council, he arose with the smile of a man about to impart wisdom, and suggested that as the clergymen of New York were always willing to lend a helping hand to charity, it would be a very clever device if they were to request the rectors of the fashionable churches to make from the altar formal announce-ment of the ball, with full particulars as to the price of tickets and the persons from whom these might be purchased. And when the night of the ball arrived at last, and Fanny Meredith was re-quested to welcome the journalists who came to ' write it up ' and to provide for their comfort,

internal and external, he said something to Harry
Brackett, who had been sent up from the 'Gotham
Gazette' to provide a picturesque description of
the ball, to be supplemented by the more personal
notes of the 'society reporter.' Just what it was
that Fanny Meredith said to Harry Brackett no
one has ever been able to ascertain exactly, but,
whatever it was, it took the journalist completely
by surprise ; he looked at the secretary of the
council for a minute in dazed astonishment, and
then, his sense of humour overcoming his indigna-
tion, he said slowly, 'Somebody must have left a
door open somewhere, and this thing blew in !'

But the petty errors the new secretary committed at the ball were as nothing to the mighty
blunder he made at the Paas dinner of the council.
The Saint Nicholas Relief Society may have any
number of annual subscribers, but it has only two
hundred members elected for life. From these two
hundred members is chosen a council of twenty-
one. Among the members are many ladies, and
at least a third of the council are of the sex which
wear ear-rings. It is this mingling of sharp men
and clever women in the council which gives its
strength to the Saint Nicholas Relief Society. In
nothing is the skill of the management shown to
more advantage than in the choice of members of
the council. There are young ladies, there are old
bachelors, there are substantial matrons, and there
are fathers of families ; and they dwell together in

unity, so far, at least, as the Saint Nicholas Relief
Society is concerned. A meeting of the council
presents a sight at once heterogeneous and charac-
teristic. Possibly it is this variety of persons and
of points of view that makes the council of the
Saint Nicholas Relief Society so successful as it
has been in its task of administering wealth and
of ministering to the needy. Certainly the dis-
similarity of character and the unity of object help
to make the annual Paas dinner a season of refresh-
ment. Most of the members of the council are
busy, but it is very rare indeed for one of them to
be absent from his seat or from her seat, as the
case may be, at the Paas dinner.

The number of the council is twenty-one, and
has always been twenty-one. Fanny Meredith
forgot all about the Paas dinner until reminded of
it less than a week before Easter. Then he rushed
off to the old-fashioned restaurant where the
dinner was always given, and he spent four hours
there in the ordering of a proper series of courses
for twenty-one people. He had seized the nearest
annual report of the society, and he gave it to a
copyist with a score of blank invitation cards, telling her to send them out to the members of the
council, in accordance with a list printed at the
end of the report. The copyist did as she was
bidden, and the invitations went forth by the
post.

But when the members of the council assembled

on the evening of the Tuesday after Easter they
were only thirteen in number. They waited nearly
an hour for the other eight, and then they sat
down ill at ease. While they were yet eating
their oysters Mr. Francis Meredith came in to gaze
on his handiwork. Mr. Jacob Leisler, jun., asked
him if he had sent all the invitations.

'Of course I did,' he answered ; 'you don't
think I could make a mistake about a little thing
like that, do you ?'

To this leading question there was no answer ;
so Meredith continued, taking a report from his
pocket :

'I wouldn't trust myself to write them, so I
gave this list to a copyist, and I put all the enve-
lopes in the post myself.'

'Let me see that report,' said Mr. Leisler,
holding out his hand. Mr. Jacob Leisler, jun., was
the chairman of the finance committee, and a man
speaking with authority. On the present occasion
he was presiding.

The unsuspecting Fanny gave him the pam-
phlet. Mr. Leisler glanced at it, read the list of
the council, turned to the date on the title-page,
and then inquired calmly :

'Mr. Meredith, do you know when this report
was printed ?'

'Last fall, of course,' answered the secretary.

'Just twenty-two years ago last fall,' Mr. Leisler
returned ; 'so if you have invited to this dinner
here to-night the council whose names appear in

this report, you have not asked the eight absent members who are alive, and you have asked eight members who are dead! And that accounts for the empty chairs here.'

Fanny Meredith laughed feebly, and then he laughed again faintly. At last he murmured, ' I seem to have made a mistake.'

As he shrank away towards the door, amid an embarrassed silence, Mr. Leisler whispered harshly to a mature and sharp-featured lady who sat at his right :

'And we seem to have made a mistake when we elected him to be secretary to the council.'

There was a general murmur of assent from the members of the council, in which nearly all joined, excepting a young old maid with frank eyes and cheerful countenance, who was sitting about half-way down the dinner-table, with a vacant seat by her side. She looked at the abashed Fanny Meredith with a compassionate smile of encouragement.

'Since you have not attended to your duty,' said Mr. Leisler severely, checking the helpless secretary on the threshold, 'since you have not seen that the other members of the council received invitations, of course they will not come —we cannot expect them. We must dine by our-selves—thirteen at table. I cannot speak for the others, but to me it is most unpleasant' to see those eight empty chairs !'

As the crestfallen Fanny Meredith retreated

hastily from the dining-room, he could not help hearing this rebuke heartily approved by the council.

II.

ALTHOUGH Mr. Jacob Leisler, jun., and Mrs. Vedder, the energetic lady on his right, and Miss Mary Van Dyne, the pleasant-faced old maid farther down on his left, and Mr. Joshua Hoffman, who sat beside her, and the rest of the thirteen members of the council who were present, saw eight empty chairs, which made awkward gaps in the company about the board—although they could count only thirteen at table, it is to be recorded that in reality these eight chairs were not empty. They were filled by those to whom the cards of invitation had been sent—the former members of the council, dead and gone in the score of years and more since the printing of the report which the new secretary had used. To the eyes of the living the eight seats were vacant. To the eyes of one who had power to see the spiritual and intangible they were occupied by those who had been bidden to the feast. How the invitations had reached their addresses no one might know, but they had been received, and they had been accepted ; and the invited guests sat at the council as they had been wont to sit there twenty-two years before. Perhaps the invitations had gone to the Dead Letter Office, and so had been forwarded to the dead whose names they bore ; perhaps they

had been taken—but speculation is idle. It
matters not how or by whom the invitations had
been delivered, there sat the ghostly guests, in
their places around the dinner-table of the council.
There they sat in the eight chairs, which to the
eye of man were empty.

It was the first time that the dead had been
bidden to this feast of the living. It was the first
time since they had laid down the burdens of this
world that they had been allowed to mingle with
their friends on earth. It was the first time—and
they feared it might be the last, and they were
eager to make the most of their good fortune. For
a long while they sat silently listening with avidity
to all stray fragments of news about those whom
they had left behind them in the land of the living.
Some of these spectral visitors had only recently
quitted this life, and perhaps they were the most
anxious to learn the sayings and doings of those
they had loved and left. Some of them had
been dead for years, and their placid faces wore a
pleasant expression of restful and comforting tran-
quillity. One of them, a handsome young fellow
in a dark blue uniform with faded shoulder-straps,
had fallen twenty-two years before in the repulse
of Pickett's charge at Gettysburg. Another had
gone down in the 'Ville de Nice' in the Bay of
Biscay in 1872. A third, a venerable man with
silvery hair and a gentle look in his soft gray eyes,
had died of old age only a few months before.

Mr. Jacob Leisler, jun., sat at the head of the

N

table, and at his right hand was Mrs. Vedder, a square-faced lady of an uncertain age, with grizzled hair and a masterful mouth. The chair on her right was apparently empty, to her evident dissatisfaction. Probably her annoyance would have been acutely increased had she been aware that the invisible occupant of this place by her side was Jesse Van Twiller, her first husband, dead these ten years or more, during eight of which she had been another man's wife.

Jesse Van Twiller had been among the earliest to arrive ; and when he found that his wife was to sit next to him he was delighted. No spook ever wore a broader smile than that which graced his features as Mrs. Vedder took her place at table by his side. But his joy was commingled with a portion of apprehension, as though he feared his wife as much as he loved her. He was a little man, of a nervous temperament, with a timid look and an expression of subdued meekness, as though he was used to be overridden by an overbearing woman. He glanced up as his former wife sat down. He seemed disconcerted when her eyes fell on him with no look of welcome recognition. For a moment he wondered if he had offended her in any way since they had parted. Then, all at once, he knew that she had not seen him : he was invisible to mortal eyes. He chafed against this condition ; he wanted her to see him and to know how glad he was to see her. To be there by her side, to be able to stretch his arm about her waist as he had done in the days of yore, to long to fold her to his heart which beat for her alone, and to be powerless as he was even to communicate to her the fact of his presence—this was most painful. The poor ghost felt that fate was hard on him. He would have given years of his spectral existence for two or three hours of human life.

These were his feelings at first. Then he wondered how she would receive him if she knew he were in her presence. He gazed at her intently as though to read her thoughts. She was older than she was when he had died—there was no doubt about that. She had the same commanding mien, the same superb port, the same majestic sweep of the arm. Yet it seemed to the man who had left her a widow that the air of domineering determination he recalled so well was not a little softened as though from want of use. 'She has missed me!' he said to himself. 'How gladly would I have her scold me now as she used to scold me so often, if only she could see me! She could not rebuke me for being late this time, but she could easily find something else to find fault about. I shouldn't care how much she bullied me, so long as I could tell her I was here. And then,' he concluded cautiously, 'if she made it too hot for me, I could be a ghost again, and she would be so surprised!'

Just then Mr. Leisler spoke to the spouse of the spook.

'I was beginning to fear that we might be deprived of your presence too, Mrs. Vedder,' he said. 'Were you not a little late ?'

Jesse Van Twiller looked at his old friend Leisler in the greatest surprise. Why had he addressed Mrs. Van Twiller as Mrs. Vedder? The first husband even turned and looked at the chair next to his, on the chance that that was occupied by the lady addressed ; but Mr. Leisler's own wife sat there. His astonishment increased as he heard his wife's answer.

'Yes,' she said, 'we were late. But it was not my fault. The doctor is a most unpunctual man.'

'The doctor?' thought Van Twiller. 'What doctor? and what had she to do with any doctor? Had she been ill? She seemed to be in robust health.'

'Dr. Vedder is a busy man,' rejoined Mr. Leisler, 'and perhaps he cannot control his time.'

So it was Dr. Vedder his wife had been waiting for. Van Twiller looked across the table at Dr. Vedder, whom he knew very well and had never liked. Dr. Vedder was a sarcastic man, with a sharp tongue, and a knack of saying disagreeable things. It was Dr. Vedder who had once asserted that Van Twiller had no more sense of humour than a hand-organ. Suddenly, with a sharp pang of jealousy, Van Twiller recalled a vague, fleeting, and half-forgotten memory of Dr. Vedder's admiration for Mrs. Van Twiller. He remembered that the doctor had once declared that he liked a masterful woman, and that Mrs. Van Twiller was

a Katherine with a poor Petruchio quite incapable
of taming her.

'That's no reason he should keep his wife
waiting,' said the former Mrs. Van Twiller plain-
tively.

'His wife!' repeated Van Twiller to himself.
'Who is his wife?'

'I was never treated in that way by my first
husband,' continued the lady.

'Her first husband!' The poor ghost shrank
back. At last he saw the change in the situation.
His wife was not his wife any more. She was the
wife of Dr. Vedder, a man whom he had disliked
always, and whom now he hated. He was seized
by a burning rage of jealousy, but he was powerless
to express his feelings. His condition was hard
to bear, for he could see, he could hear, he could
suffer, and he could do nothing.

As Van Twiller was thinking this out hotly,
the sharp voice of Dr. Vedder stabbed him suddenly.

'I have noticed,' remarked the doctor, who was
seated exactly opposite his wife's first husband,
'that a woman always thinks more highly of a man
after he is dead and gone. She is ready enough
to praise him when it is too late for the commendation to comfort him. I believe a widow doubly
cherishes the memory of a hen pecked husband.'

With the suave smile of a conscious peace-
maker, who sees possible offence in a speech, Mr.
Leisler said, 'You are hard on the widows,
Doctor.'

'Not at all,' the doctor answered, with a dry little wrinkle at the corners of his mouth, 'not at all. I am a scientific observer, making logical deductions from a multitude of facts. To the man who lives out West, the only good Indian is a dead Indian ; so to the widow, the only good husband is the dead husband ! '

'I'm sure,' cried Mrs. Vedder indignantly, 'that Mr. Van Twiller would never have said anything like that.'

'Certainly not,' her husband replied. 'Van Twiller couldn't, for Van Twiller wasn't a scientific observer.'

A covert sneer in Dr. Vedder's tone as he said this cut little Van Twiller to the soul, and again he longed for material hands that he might clutch his rival by the throat. At the thought of his absolute inability to do aught for himself, he shivered with despair.

It was perhaps some frigid emanation from Van Twiller which affected Mrs. Vedder's nerves, for she shuddered slightly before replying to her husband.

'It is not for us to bandy words now about Mr. Van Twiller's attainments,' she remarked deliberately. 'He was truly a gentleman, with all the mildness of a gentleman, quite incapable of giving any one a harsh word or a cross look.'

'In fact he had absolutely no faults at all,' said Dr. Vedder sarcastically. But if he could then have seen the expression on the pallid face of

his predecessor, he would have been in a position
to contradict his wife's last assertion.

' He had very few indeed ! ' replied his wife ;
' in my eyes he was perfect ! '

She paused for a second, and Van Twiller
wished that she had believed in his perfection
while he was alive. Then she added bitterly,
' To know him was to love him ! '

The dry little wrinkle returned to the corners
of Dr. Vedder's mouth as he answered quietly,
'Perhaps so—I didn't know him well ! '

And again the poor ghost writhed in invisible
anguish, utterly helpless to resent the insult.

' I remember Mr. Van Twiller distinctly,' remarked Mr. Leisler blandly ; ' he was an easy-
going and good-natured man, with a kind word for
everybody.'

' In fact, he was everybody's friend,' Dr. Vedder
returned, ' and nobody's enemy but his own. His
best quality in my eyes is that he is not here to-
night.'

The doctor could not know that the little man
at whom he was girding was separated from him
by the breadth of the table only, and was suffering
with his whole being as every sneer reached its
mark far more surely than he who shot the chance
arrow could guess.

' You are bitter,' said Mr. Leisler easily ; ' I fear
you are a misanthrope.'

The doctor laughed a little, and answered, 'No,
I'm not exactly a misanthrope or even a miso-

gynist, but I have ceased to be philanthropic since I discovered that man is descended from a monkey.'

Mrs. Vedder was about to make a hasty reply to this, when she caught the doctor's eye. To the surprise of Van Twiller, she hesitated, checked herself suddenly, and said nothing. He wondered how it was that his wife had changed; he knew that she had never quailed before his eye; and he found himself doubting whether he would not have preferred to see her show her old spirit. He saw that she was sadly tamed now; and he marvelled why he should regret the quenching of her fiery spirit. She did not seem the same to him, and he missed the old mastery to which he was accustomed. This blunted the joy of the meeting he had anticipated hopefully ever since he had received the invitation. His wife was no longer his. She was not even the woman he had loved, honoured, and obeyed for years. The poor ghost felt lonelier than he had ever felt before. He began to regret that he had been permitted again to come on earth.

A waiter had filled Dr. Vedder's glass. He took it in his hand. 'No,' he said, 'I'm not a philanthropist; I take no stock in the aggressive optimism of the sentimentalists. In fact, I suppose I'm a persistent pessimist. What is my fellow-man to me—or my fellow-woman either?'

Mr. Jacob Leisler, jun., was not a man whose perceptions were fine or quick, but he was moved to resent clumsily the offensiveness of these words.

'But your wife——' he began.

'Oh, my wife!' interrupted Dr. Vedder; 'my wife and I are one, you know.'

Van Twiller looked at Mrs. Vedder to see how she would take this. She said nothing. She smiled acidly. It was not doubtful that she was greatly changed.

'I try to shape my course by the doctrine of enlightened selfishness,' continued the doctor. 'Let us enjoy life while we may. Eat, drink, and be merry, for to-morrow we die. In the struggle for existence the fittest survive and the weakest are weeded out—and so much the better!'

Both Mrs. Vedder and Mr. Leisler made ready to reply, when the doctor suddenly went on, sharpening his voice to its keenest edge:

'So much the better for him! Your dead man is your happy man. He has no enemies, and even his widow praises him—especially if she has re-married. In fact, he has all the virtues, now he has no use for any of them.' Then the doctor raised his glass. 'The toast of the English in India suggests true wisdom, after all:

"Ho! stand to your glasses steady!
  The world is a world of lies;
A cup to the dead already,
  And hurrah for the next man that dies!"

Mr. Leisler drew himself up with dignity and

addressed the doctor with a stiff severity of manner :

'I am surprised, Dr. Vedder, that you should express such views of life on such an occasion as this. I confess I do not hold with you at all. I——'

'You cannot lure me into a debate at dinner,' the doctor answered, as Mr. Leisler paused for fit words to express his complicated feelings. 'I never get into a discussion at table, for the man who isn't hungry always has the best of the argument.'

The unfortunate spook, forced to listen to this unmannerly talk of the man who had married his widow, sat silent and abashed. He knew not what to think. He did not recognise his wife. When he was alive she had been full of fiery vigour and of undaunted spirit. He would never have dared to address her thus boldly and to brave the wrath which was wont to flame out, at odd moments, like forked lightning. In dumb wonder he waited for her swift protest ; but she said nothing ; whereat he marvelled not a little.

Mr. Leisler asked himself why Dr. Vedder was unusually disagreeable this evening, for the doctor was a clever man and could make a pleasant impression when he chose. With the hope of turning the talk into a more cheerful channel Mr. Leisler addressed Mrs. Vedder.

'Isn't Miss Van Dyne looking very well to-night ?' he asked.

Mrs. Vedder looked down the table at the cheery and young-looking old maid.

'Yes,' she answered, after a moment's hesitation, 'she seems almost happy ; but then, she is not married.'

'She has been faithful to the memory of her lost love,' said Mr. Leisler. 'Let me see—how many years is it now since Captain De Ruyter was killed at Gettysburg ?'

'You don't mean to tell me that you believe that a woman has been in love with a dead man for twenty-two years, do you ?' Dr. Vedder asked with an incredulous smile.

'Why not ?' returned his wife.

The doctor evaded an answer to this direct question. 'If your diagnosis is right, she has had a dull enough time of it,' he said. 'And she has nothing to show for her devotion.'

'Virtue is its own reward,' Mr. Leisler remarked judicially.

'But love isn't,' the doctor replied. 'Love is like this champagne,' and he raised his glass ; 'it is very sparkling when it is young, but as it gets older it loses its flavour.' He emptied the glass and set it down. 'And if one is all alone with it, there may be a headache the next morning.'

'What has made you so sarcastic this evening ?' asked Mr. Leisler.

'I don't know,' Dr. Vedder answered. 'I am in company with evil spirits, I think. If I were a believer in such things, I should say that I was subject to an adverse influence. And I was all right when I came. Perhaps it is this wretched dinner.'

Perhaps it was the dinner, but little Van Twiller was conscious of a throb of ill-natured joy at the thought that it was possibly his presence, all unknown as it was, which had thus disturbed the equanimity of the doctor and revealed his lower nature. He looked at Mrs. Vedder, and he saw she was eating her dinner slowly and in silence, with a stiffening of the muscles of the face—a sign he had recognised readily enough.

'After all,' continued the doctor, 'these are the two great banes of man's existence—dyspepsia and matrimony.'

'Come, come,' Mr. Leisler said cheerfully, 'you must not abuse marriage ; it is the chief end of life.'

'It was very nearly the end of mine,' returned Dr. Vedder ; 'I caught such a cold in the church that I have not been into one since.'

Just then one of the waiters came to Mr. Leisler with a request that he should change his place for a little while, and take his seat at the other end of the table, where there was a vacant chair. Glad of an excuse to get away from a man in ill-humour, Mr. Leisler apologised to Mrs. Vedder and withdrew to join his other friends.

Van Twiller saw a red spot burning brightly on Mrs. Vedder's cheek, and he knew that this was another danger-signal.

She bent forward towards her husband, and in a low voice, trembling a little with suppressed ire, she hissed across the table, 'I see what you are after! But you will not succeed. I can keep my temper though I bite my tongue out. It takes two to quarrel, remember!'

'It takes two to get married,' retorted Dr. Vedder, 'so that proves nothing.'

For the first time the poor ghost saw his wife's eyes fill with tears.

'Mr. Van Twiller never treated me so,' she said hurriedly. 'I wish he were alive now!'

The dry little wrinkle came back to the corners of the doctor's mouth, but he made no reply.

Little Van Twiller looked from one to the other, as they stared at each other. Then he said to himself, sighing softly:

'Well, well, perhaps it is better as it is!'

III.

MISS MARY VAN DYNE was sitting almost in the centre of one side of the long dinner-table. At her right was Mr. Joshua Hoffman, a man whose heart was as large as his purse was long, and who kept both open to the call of the suffering. At her left was a vacant chair—or what seemed so to the eyes of the living men and women at the table. They did not know that it was occupied by Remsen de Ruyter, whose maiden widow Mary Van Dyne had held herself to be ever since a bullet had reached his heart on the heights of Gettysburg. For nearly twenty-two years now she had lived on, alone in the world, but never lonely, for she had given herself up to good works.   Her presence was welcome in the children's ward of every hospital, and the love of these little ones nourished her soul and sustained her spirit.   Between her and Joshua Hoffman there were bonds of sympathy, and they had many things in common.   The good old man was very fond of the brave little woman who had tried to turn her private sorrow to the benefit of the helpless and the innocent.

They were glad to find themselves side by side at table, and they talked to each other with interest.

'You are not really old, Mr. Hoffman,' she was saying; 'you look very young yet.   To-night I wouldn't give you fifty!'

'My dear young lady, you haven't fifty to give,' he answered with a smile; 'and if you had, why I should then have a hundred and twenty-five— which is more than my share of years.'

'You are not really seventy-five?' she asked.

'Really, I am seventy-five.   I am a past-due coupon, as I heard one of the boys saying on the street the other day,' returned Joshua Hoffman, with a smile as pleasant as hers.

'And how old am I?' she inquired.

'Whatever your age is,' he answered, 'to-night you do not look it!'

'Shall I arise and curtsey for that?' she asked, blushing with pleasure at his courtly compliment. 'You see I like to be flattered still, although I am an old maid of two-score years.'

'Really now, my child,' said the old man, 'you are not forty? Let me see—it does not seem so very long ago since he came and told me how happy he was because you had promised to marry him. Does it pain you to talk of him now?'

'I think of him always, day and night. Why should I not be glad to talk about him with you whom he loved, and to whom he owed so much?'

'He was a good boy,' Joshua Hoffman continued in his kindly voice. 'I can recall the day he told me about you; it was a fine, clear morning in early spring.'

'It was the 16th of May, 1863,' she said simply. 'He had asked me to marry him the night before, and he said that you were the first he would tell.'

'He was a good boy, and a brave boy, and he died like a man,' said the old man gently. Then he relapsed into silence as his thoughts went back to the dark days of the war.

Miss Mary Van Dyne was also thinking of the past. Unconsciously she lived again in her youth when she first saw Remsen de Ruyter, a bright handsome boy, scarcely older than she was: he was only twenty-one when he died. They had loved each other from the first, although it was a whole long winter before he had dared to tell her —a long winter of delicious doubt and fearful ecstasy. She recalled all the circumstances of his avowal of his love, and her cheeks burned as she thought of the gush of unspeakable joy which had filled her heart as he folded her in his arms for the first time.   She remembered how, two nights after, before they had told the news to any one but her mother and his benefactor Joshua Hoffman, she sat next to him at this annual dinner of the council of the Saint Nicholas Relief Society; they were the very youngest members, and it was the first time they had been asked.   So strong was the rush of memory of the happy scene, that she gave a quick glance at the place on her left, as though half-expecting to see him seated there still.   And there he was by her side, although she could not see him now.

He was there, but he could not speak to her ; he could not tell her of his presence ; he could not tell her how he loved her still, and more than ever. It was hard.   Yet he was glad to be by her side, to see her, to look into her frank face, to gaze on her noble eyes.

And she felt comforted she knew not why, as though by an invisible presence.   Her heart was lifted up.   Although the grass had woven a green blanket over his grave for now more than twenty years, he did not seem so far from her.   She hoped she would not have so long to wait before she might join him, never again to be parted.   Then her thoughts turned to the last time she had seen him, the morning his regiment had left New York for the front.   It was a beautiful day early in June when he came to bid her farewell for the last time. They talked all the morning seriously and hope-

fully. Then the hour came at last, and all too soon.
She bore herself bravely ; without a tear she kissed
him and held him in her arms for a minute, and
bade him go. She watched him as he walked
away. How well she could recall everything
which her senses had noted unconsciously during
the two minutes before he paused at the corner of
the street to wave his hand before he vanished for
ever. There were roses beginning to blow in the
little bit of green before the house ; there was a
hand-organ in the next street from which faint
strains of 'John Brown's Body' came over the
house-tops ; the noon whistle of a neighbouring fac-
tory suddenly broke the silence as he blew her a
kiss, and went out of her sight to his death. Then
she had been able to get to her room somehow—
she never knew how—and to throw herself on her
bed before she broke down.

The memory was bitter and sweet, but never
before had it been as sweet. She turned her eyes
on the vacant chair by her side, and involuntarily
she reached out her hand. It grasped nothing, it
felt nothing, yet her fingers tingled as with a shock
of joy. She gazed at the empty chair again in
charmed wonder. She could not tell what subtle
influence of peace and comfort enveloped her as she
mused upon the past with her arm resting on the
chair beside her. Then her glance fell on a card
beside the plate, and with a sudden suffusion of
the eyes she read his name. The new secretary of
the council had used the list of twenty-two years

O

before, and again his place had been set beside
hers.   The tears which veiled her sight hid the
empty chair from her for a minute, and if she
turned her head she might almost fancy that he
was seated there.   It was a fancy only, but it
pleased her to indulge in it.   It brought back the
happy past.   It brought him back, almost, for a
fleeting minute.

And he, as he sat there, could make no sign.
With the keen intuition of love, he read her
thoughts in her face.   He knew that she was thinking of him, and that in the thought of him she was
happy again.

And thus the long dinner drew to an end at
last.

When the president gave the signal for the
withdrawal into another room that the usual business meeting of the council might take place, the
members rose together.   Joshua Hoffman was
silent, as though he divined her mood and sympa-
thetically respected it.   He offered her his arm,
and she took it, looking back regretfully, with a
longing and lingering gaze, at the place where they
had sat side by side.

IV.

As the living members of the council left the
dining-room, the ghostly guests gathered together
to talk over what they had seen and heard.   Only
Remsen de Ruyter was silent; his feelings were

too sacred to find vent in words. He alone wore a smile of consolation and comfort. The rest chattered along in tumultuous conversation.

'It has been a strange experience,' said the very old gentleman—'a very strange experience.'

'More painful than pleasant, I think,' little Van Twiller remarked. —

'I thought we had been invited as a compliment,' said another of the ghosts discontentedly, 'but it seems it was all a mistake of the new secretary—Fanny Meredith, they call him.'

'Excellent young man!' the old gentleman declared with emphasis—' an excellent young man; so thoughtful of him; so considerate of the feelings of his elders. I shall accept his invitation next year.'

'So shall I!' added several voices.

'Oh, I'll come too,' said Jesse Van Twiller. 'I want to see what will happen next.'

Only Remsen de Ruyter said nothing.

V.

But long before the next annual dinner of the council of the Saint Nicholas Relief Society, the resignation of Mr. Francis Meredith had been requested, and in his stead there had been elected a secretary of more trustworthy habits; and the new secretary was very particular in sending out the invitations to the next annual dinner.

So the poor ghosts never had another chance

If they had been asked again, there would have been one more of them, for ten days after the dinner which Fanny Meredith had so miserably mismanaged Dr. Vedder died suddenly.

The new secretary took great pains also in the ordering of the dinner, and in the arranging of the guests. His efforts were rewarded; there was general satisfaction expressed by the members of the council; and he was congratulated on the most successful dinner ever given. Amid the pervading gaiety of the occasion there was only one guest who regretted the dinner of the year before. This was Miss Mary Van Dyne. She said nothing about it to any one; indeed, she was accustomed to keep her feelings to herself. But she missed an inexplicable something which had made the other dinner the most delightful memory of her later life.

ESTHER FEVEREL

ESTHER FEVEREL.

ABOUT a mile beyond the straggling outskirts of a New England village once as young and energetic as any in the land, but to-day so old and exhausted that it seems to have sunk into restful sleep, there stands a house built of dull gray stone, and bearing bravely still the onslaught of the New England winters it has withstood for now nearly two centuries. This house, beginning at last to bear witness to the wear of time, is one of the oldest in America; it is one of the few buildings of the seventeenth century which survive to this last quarter of the nineteenth. To us who live in an age of rush and glitter the appearance of the house is in no wise remarkable except for its evident antiquity; nor should we turn aside now to consider what the contemporaries of the first owner were wont to call the stately nobility of its proportions. But our eyes are not the eyes of the early colonists of New England, and the stone house which Judge Feverel built was long a wonder for miles around. More than one fast-day sermon had been directed against its magnificence, which seemed out of place amid the humble beginnings of the growing colony.

There yet lingered a tradition that the house had
once been called 'The Judge's Folly.' But the
nickname had died away long ago as the magnificence of the house had faded. And as time, un-
hasting and unresting, sped slowly, the house of
the stern and fiery Roger Feverel had fallen from
grace, and the fortunes of the elder branch of the
Feverels were fallen with it.

As the late November sun sent its declining
rays across the low Western hills, and gilded the
substantial chimney which rose above the slant
roof of the house which Judge Feverel had built,
a man on horseback drew rein before the door.
He looked at the house like one who had never
seen it before ; but his face lighted up at once with
a glance of recognition and a smile of satisfaction
that he had come to the end of his travels at last,
and reached a haven of rest. He sprang from his
horse, which he tethered to a post at the edge of
the path. He was a handsome young fellow—for
young he was yet, in spite of his having already
accomplished half of a man's allotted span of life.
He had dark wavy hair, quick black eyes, and a
frank face, on which there might be seen at times
a dreamy look. His walk indicated a resolute
self-reliance, and he passed up the unfamiliar path
as though he had a right to be there.

As he stood on the low step before the door of
the house, after ringing the bell, he turned to look
at the little garden which surrounded the house,
and at the few scant fields which were attached to

it ; then he raised his head with a little touch of pride as he recalled the time when the owner of the house was the owner also of the land for a mile or more on every side of it. One by one these broad acres had slipped from the loose hands of the Feverels, and generation after generation the Feverels had become poorer and poorer, as though there had been a curse on them and on their house.

'On this house there may be a curse, and there is reason for it,' thought John Feverel, as he stood for the first time at the door of the home of the Feverels ; ' but the curse, if curse there be, is on this house only, and not on the Feverels at large. It is on them, perhaps, who remain here and keep up the flame of hatred, but it is not on those who have gone forth into the world. There was no curse on my grandfather when he, the younger son, went out from here and prospered, while the elder son remained here and saw his substance shrivel up. There was no curse on my father, who made his way in the world without hindrance from ill fortune. There is no curse on me as yet. Standing here on the threshold of the house of the Feverels, I can look back over my past with pleasure, for I have been happier than most men, and I can look forward to the future with hope.'

Receiving no answer to his repeated ring, John Feverel rapped sharply on the panel of the door Under the force of the blow, the door opened silently, and disclosed a broad hall, at the farther

end of which, facing the entrance, there was a
large fire-place, where a few sticks of wood were
burning brightly.   The visitor stood for a moment
on the door-step, as though awaiting an invitation
to enter.   Then he walked into the house and
looked about him.   The hall was spacious, old-
fashioned, quaint.   The wood-work had reached a
stage of decay when care could no longer conceal
the marks of age and use.   Everything was clean
and worn-out.   The tidiness and neatness, the
nosegay of fresh flowers in a vase by a window,
the little touches of colour elsewhere, revealed a
woman's hand.   Yet the house seemed to be
empty.   There was no one to welcome John
Feverel to the home of his ancestors.

'Uncle Timothy,' he called.   'Cousin Esther!'
But there came no answer.   The house was as
deserted as it was desolate.   From its stillness it
might be a habitation of the dead, where no one
dwelt but the ghosts of the past.

He called again, and again he received no
reply.

Neither of his kinsfolk was at home to greet
him.   And yet it was to see them almost as much
as to take possession of the property that he had
cut short his travels and crossed the ocean in
haste.

John Feverel was the grandson of a John
Feverel who left this Eastern home of the family
to seek his fortune in the West.   In this under-
taking he had prospered as no Feverel before him

had prospered since the fire had first smoked on the hearth of ' The Judge's Folly.' He worked and made money : he married and saw his children grow up about him ; and in his old age he rested in peace before he died happily. His son, John Feverel again, made yet another move to the West, and he prospered as his father had prospered. When he died he left to his only son, the John Feverel who now stood in the hall of the house built by Roger Feverel nearly two hundred years ago, three good things : a brave heart, a keen head, and a modest fortune. To these John Feverel added a quality of his own, an inquiring mind ever athirst for knowledge. He put his wits to work and did not cease from labour until he had doubled the fortune left him by his father. Although he was then barely thirty-five years of age, and although he saw before him the prospect of great riches, he gave up his business and rested satisfied with the comfortable competence he had attained. He felt that he had a more important work in life than the mere making of money. Just what this future work might be he did not know, but he was ready to undertake whatever seemed to him fit and worthy. In the meanwhile he set about improving himself by travel. He had more than his share of that mysticism of the West which matches so curiously with the occult temperament of the Orient. Even as a boy he had become an adept in the cabalistic secrets of the Rosicrucians. As a man he travelled throughout the East, seeking to sate his desire to gaze on strange things, and to penetrate the obscure mysteries of strange people. He had sought to discover the means whereby the wonder-workers of the East wrought their miracles. He was learned in the lore of the alchemists, and he had traversed Arabia in search of the surviving repositories of their recondite wisdom. To all that he saw he applied his shrewd commonsense. The results of his experiment and investigation he kept to himself ; but he walked among men as one who has peered deep into the enigmas of life and pondered upon them long and earnestly.

It may be that, for a little space, he stood in danger of sinking into the lethargy of Buddhistic contemplation. He was far up in the Himalayas when he received a letter which suddenly recalled him to a sharp self-consciousness. It was from Esther Feverel, the only daughter of Timothy Feverel, the last survivor of the elder branch of the old Judge's family. It told him in few and simple words that her father's affairs were hopelessly involved, and that a mortgage on the old house was about to be foreclosed ; and it suggested that perhaps he might like to buy it, so that the house should still be owned by a Feverel. John Feverel had never seen any of his New England relatives, and he had given them little thought ; but with the old house, with the strange story of its building, and with the legends which clustered about its hearth, he was perfectly familiar. He had sat by his grandfather's knee, night after night—

during the festival reunions which brought together the various members of the Western branch of the family—and he had treasured up every word which fell from his grandfather's lips, when he told of 'The Judge's Folly,' and of the fire on its hearth, and of the ill fortune which followed the house and its inmates. To have the house pass into his possession was a boon he had not dared to hope for.

The letter which informed him that its purchase was possible was written in the name of Timothy Feverel, but the hand was the hand of his daughter. John Feverel had studied chirography as he had studied whatever else might serve to increase his knowledge of men. He was wont to read character by handwriting with a success often startling to himself. The symbols of character he deciphered in the sincere handwriting of Esther Feverel made him wish to meet her and know more of her.

He wrote to her at once, venturing to call her cousin, and telling her that he had given orders to have the place bought for him whenever the mortgagee saw fit to foreclose. Furthermore, assuming the liberty of a kinsman, he begged that she and her father would continue to live in the house as before, taking care of it for him, against the time when he should return to America.

A few months later, when he had begun to be weary of his years of wandering in search of the unknowable, he had received another letter from Esther, letting him know that the sale had taken place, and that the house was his, and thanking him for the kindness extended to her father and herself—a kindness of which they would gladly avail themselves until his return. So gentle was this letter, so sweet in its maidenly modesty, so frank and womanly was it, so charming was the character revealed by its chirography, that it wrought a change in John Feverel's views of life. He abandoned a daring trip to the chief temples of China, and made his way back to America.

Now, as he stood for the first time in the home of the Feverels, he had a sharp feeling of disappointment that Esther was not there to bid him welcome. Before he had paced the hall half a dozen times, this feeling gave way, and he began even to be glad that he was alone, and that his first impressions of the old house might be pure of all admixture of the opinions of another, even were that other his cousin Esther. So accurate had been his grandfather's description, and so retentive had been his own memory, that he felt at home in the house as soon as he entered the door. He gazed from the windows, and the view was to him as though he had seen it before in some former existence. The tall clock on the stairs looked down on him as benignantly as it had looked down on the other children of the family in the two centuries since it first began to measure eternity into time. The mirror over the mantel-piece at the end of the hall reflected his image as it had reflected the image of eight generations of Feverels since the old Judge set it against the chimney. The ancient

chair before the fire extended its arms as hospi-
tably to him as it had to his great-grandfather,
the last of his line who had sat in it.   On John
Feverel these things had a strange effect; he felt
as though he had come home at last—and for the
first time.

As he sat himself down in the chair before the
fire and glanced up at the mirror, he saw an expression on his face he had never known there before.   He had a strange presentiment that he was
at the turning-point of his career.   It was as
though he were halting at the threshold of a new
life, pausing for a moment to look back across the
past, and yet regarding the future hopefully.   He
lowered his eyes, and they fell on the date carven
deep into the heavy timbers of the mantel-piece—
1692.   For nearly two hundred years had the fire
been alight on that hearth day and night, winter
and summer, year after year.   There the flame had
burned and smouldered and blazed since the Judge,
in his fanaticism and wrath, had brought home a
brand from the burning of a poor wretch whom he
had sentenced to death for an abhorrent crime of
petty treason.   On that hearth, beneath the faded
tiles, whereon were depicted Cain and Abel, David
and Goliath, Sisera and Jael, and other characters
in Biblical scenes of bloodshed, the fire had never
ceased rising and falling since Roger Feverel had
kindled it for the first time with a brand from the
burning, that it might be an enduring witness to
his righteousness, and that it should be ready at all

times in the future to fire the torch whenever the
same awful vengeance might need to be taken once
again.   Roger Feverel was dead and buried, and
the hatreds and the beliefs and the heresies of his
time were dead and buried also, but the fire he
kindled was still smoking on his hearth.   Roger
Feverel's son and his grandson and his great-grand-
son had passed away, one after another ; but the fire
that the founder of the family had lighted when he
built the house lived on, and was as young as ever.
Generation followed generation to the grave, but
the fire of intolerance still burned on its altar as
though Roger Feverel had made a covenant with
his descendants that they should feed the flame for
ever.   So strongly had the traditions of the family
seized John Feverel that he bent forward and laid
across the embers two pieces from the piles of cut
wood ready to his hand on either side of the fire-
place.

As he lay back again in the chair he saw in the
mirror the reflection of his smile, for he was half
conscious that his humorous scepticism mated ill
with the fanatic intolerance of the old Judge who
had set light to that fire.   He wondered whether
Roger Feverel had also looked into the mirror as
he heaped fuel upon the flame.   No doubt the
Judge had seen the look on his own dark face,
though he knew not how to read its meaning.   The
glass had hung there since the fire first flamed.   In
it had been reflected the life history of the Feverels.
Across the surface of that frail glass had passed the

image of the pride and the joys and the sorrows
of Roger Feverel and of his descendants. It had
seen their youth and their old age ; it had seen
their sufferings, and it may be their death. It had
been a silent witness to their prosperity, and, after
many years, to their poverty, but never to their
disgrace or their shame, for they always held their
heads high, and their poverty was never tarnished
with dishonour.

As John Feverel sat in the chair before the fire
and gazed up into the mirror he thought of these
things, and he wished that these scenes might be
evoked from the past, and shown again in the glass
wherein they had been reflected as they happened.
He wondered what the Judge would have thought
of the magic mirrors of Japan, in which a vanished
scene may be made to reappear. Surely the Judge
would have seen nothing strange in the tale, but
he would have been prompt to punish any man
who should make use of such a device of the devil.

John Feverel recalled the temple on the flanks
of Fusiyama wherein the Japanese priests preserved
jealously the most potent of these magic mirrors.
It was in this temple that—by one of those curious
reproductions in strange countries of the rites and
mysteries of ancient civilisation—a perpetual fire
was cherished on the altar, guarded night and day,
as the virgins of Roma kept up the sacred flame of
Vesta. When a certain mysteriously compounded
preparation was thrown upon this fire, a dense
smoke arose and veiled the magic mirror, which

P

hung just above the altar, and it was through the dim haze of this smoke that the pictures of the past became visible in the glass.

Suddenly John Feverel sprang to his feet. It had struck him that here in 'The Judge's Folly' in New England there was an ever-burning fire beneath a mirror just as there was in the Japanese temple on the side of Fusiyama. And at the same time he remembered that he had begged and bribed a priest of the temple to give him a portion of the preparation thrown upon the fire beneath the magic mirror. With infinite precaution the priest had confided it to him, incased in a tiny silver ball, the surface of which was curiously wrought with a mystic device. This ball, the contents of which he had intended to submit to chemical analysis whenever occasion served, he had worn ever since attached to his watch-chain as a charm. As he thought of it his fingers closed upon it, and the worn links of the chain parted and left the ball in his hand. It was as though the inanimate thing had whispered to him that the time had come when it could be of use.

Obeying an impulse which he felt to be well-nigh irresistible, John Feverel drew forward the scattered fragments of the fire which had burned on that hearth for nearly twice a hundred years. Then, with a single turn of his wrist, he twisted apart the silver hemispheres which contained the magical compound of the Japanese temple. A white powder fell from them upon the glowing

embers, a pungent aroma filled the air, and a thick
smoke arose, veiling the mirror from view. As
the cool evening breeze, playing through the open
door, caused the cloud of smoke to waver and shift
from side to side, John Feverel, reclining in the
chair before the fire, felt as one looking through a
glass darkly. Figures, dim and indistinct, seemed
to be visible in the mirror, into which he peered
resolutely, calling up the past with the whole force
of his will. He sat motionless, and gave himself
up to the spell. His whole being was attuned in
harmony with the moment. Whether it was
memory, or imagination aided by memory, or
whether the charm had veritably some occult
potency, mattered little. As he gazed into the
mirror through the circling smoke which rose
steadily from the fire beneath he saw visions, and
in time they took form and colour. Some scenes
stood out more vividly than others, to John
Feverel's delight, for he soon found that he saw
more clearly what he was most familiar with, and
what he most wished to see, as though the mirror
responded to some secret sympathy of his soul.
He beheld the three sons of the house of Feverel,
the brothers of Esther, dead before she was born,
boys all three of them, but manly and full of spirit;
he saw them come to bid farewell to their mother,
as they went forth, clad in dark blue, musket on
shoulder, on the long march which should end only
with their death, one on the plains of Virginia, and
one in the bayous of Louisiana, and one on the hill

at Gettysburg ; and the shot which killed this last reached the heart of the mother, and was fatal, though she lingered long enough to clasp her little daughter in her arms before she followed her boys across the dark threshold of death.

Then a thick cloud of smoke rolled across the mirror, as though a volley had been fired over their graves, and as this drifted away, John Feverel, looking fixedly in the glass, saw the open door of the house, and a little maid went forth and gave a glass of water to a courtly old gentleman, who remained uncovered before her while he quenched his thirst. He knew that the little maid was his grandfather's sister, and he recognised the courtly old gentleman as one who had come to bring us help in time of direst need, and who was, many years later, on a visit to America as the guest of the nation.

As this pleasant vision faded away softly and was resolved into nothing, there fell upon the ear of the man who was peering into the mirror, with all his faculties at their utmost tension—there fell upon his ear as it had been a rattle of drums, and he saw a company of redcoats drawn up before the house, and on the door-step, confronting them sturdily, whilst she patted the babe at her breast, stood the beautiful Rachel Feverel, wife of Colonel Francis Feverel, parleying with the captain of the British troops, and bandying words with him pertly, that he might delay, all to give the Continentals time to rally and return and cut them off.

While he looked the scene changed, and the rattle of drums was drowned by shrieks and shrill yells like the cries of wild beasts. The door was closed and barred, and defended by half a score of strong men. The stanch shutters of the windows were firmly fastened, and men were firing through the loop-holes. Fiery-headed arrows fell against the door now and again, and were extinguished just as they were about to fire the house. But though the painted Indians encompassed them on every side, and escape was impossible, and death was waiting for them, and a fate worse than death, the women of the family were not craven ; some of them were loading the muskets, every shot from which hit the living mark it was aimed at ; and some were gathered in a group about the fire, melting lead from the roof and running it into bullet-moulds. A little of the water into which the hot bullets were dropped fell upon the roaring logs on the hearth, and the white steam rushed up and bedimmed the mirror so that John Feverel could see nothing more for a long while.

At last the steam and the smoke parted again and left the glass clear. The hall was silent and deserted ; and Roger Feverel paced slowly and thoughtfully up and down, from the hearth he had lighted with a brand from the burning he had decreed, to the door which shut out the glory of the summer sun. Judge Feverel was not an old man even then, though he had aged since the day when he had done his duty at Hadley fight, by the

side and under the orders of the gray warrior who
came forth mysteriously to lead the colonists to
victory, and who was recognised as Goffe the
regicide.   As he strode up and down the hall of
'The Judge's Folly' he did not note a light foot-
step upon the stair, and he did not see a slight and
graceful girlish figure, until his daughter stole her
arm in his as he turned on his heel near the door.
When Roger Feverel felt her gentle touch his hard
face softened, and he gave her a look of deep affection mingled with solicitude.   John Feverel recalled the family tradition of the Judge's daughter,
who began to sicken and fade as soon as she set
foot in the house her father had built ; she was his
favourite of all his children, in so far at least as his
stern justice allowed him to make any distinction
between them.   As she leaned on her father's arm
she seemed so fragile that a puff of the winter
breeze would blow her away, and it was true that
she did not live out the first December in the new
house.   She turned with her father and drew near
the fire, and for the first time her face became visible
to John Feverel.   He looked at her with surprise,
for he recognised her—at least he had a vague
feeling that he had beheld her face before.   The
beautiful mouth, the tender eyes, the delicate wave
of the hair drawn tightly back, were familiar to
him, like a face seen in a dream.   There came a
sudden thickening of the misty vapour which en-
wrapped the mirror, and for a moment he seemed
to see her image upon this unsubstantial curtain ;

and then he remembered where it was that he had
first beheld the face of the Judge's daughter, and
he knew it was the face of his promised bride.

A year before, John Feverel had been in Egypt,
and one day he had joined a little party who
wished to view the Sphinx by night. After the
pale green sunset had died away, and the ruddy
after-glow had followed it swiftly, and the short
twilight had given place to the darkness of night,
the party sat around a fire before the house where .
they were to sleep. While John Feverel was lying
on the sand, under the shadow of the Sphinx,
musing on the riddle of life, he was suddenly
awakened to the emptiness of existence by the
arrival of a little band of strolling performers, one
of whom, apparently a Hindoo, and a man of
unusual skill and presence, performed the cus-
tomary wonders of the itinerant magician. A
dragoman hinted to one of the party that this
Hindoo had great powers, and that he had been
known to reveal to a man the portrait of his future
bride. John Feverel, who had drawn on one side,
took no part in the clamorous outcry of his fellow-
travellers for an immediate exhibition of his peculiar power, and he was much surprised when the
Hindoo turned to him gravely and offered to work
the wonder for him, and for him alone. With his
keen interest in thaumaturgy, Feverel accepted the
offer. The Hindoo made two smaller fires equi-
distant from that around which the travellers sat,
and at each he stationed one of the two boys who

served as his assistants. Then the Hindoo looked into John Feverel's hand and studied its lines for a moment. Producing a package of some strange Oriental incense, he bade Feverel cast a handful of it on the fire. As he obeyed, a thick column of smoke shot into the air, and in the centre of this column he saw a woman's face. It was the same face he was to see again in the mirror.

It was a face he could now never more forget. It had been revealed to him twice in a vision, once in a column of smoke in Egypt, and once again in a mirror here in New England. He wondered if he was never to behold her in more tangible reality, and to meet her face to face in actual life, where he might take her by the hand and bid her mark the beatings of his heart, and ask her to share his life through good fortune and ill.

He sat silently and long, dreaming and musing. When he aroused himself at last, the rising smoke was now only a thin thread, and the fire had shrivelled to a few scant embers. He had a sus-picion that there was some ingredient in the Japanese preparation he had sprinkled over the flames which had sufficed to quench them finally. For the first time in the two centuries since Roger Feverel had lighted the fire on that hearth it burned low, and although it yet lingered and might be re-suscitated by effort, it was well-nigh dead. Through the open door the slant rays of the setting sun en-tered the hall and bathed it in an immaterial glory.

John Feverel raised his eyes again to the mirror to see if haply he might gain another glimpse of the face which had moved him so strangely. The glass was no longer wreathed in vapour, and yet again it reflected the same face, not dimly now, nor indistinct, not as a phantom, intangible and tantalizing, but alive, and with the smile of life and health and youth. Then he heard a light footfall, and he sprang to his feet and stood before the woman of his vision. And she stood before him in flesh and blood, this woman whom he had seen only in the mirror of the past. Mouth and eyes and hair, and the beauty of which these were symbols, were to him unmistakable. Even her dress in its simplicity recalled that of Roger Feverel's daughter. The beauty which in the evanescent visions had been vague and fleeting was in life beyond all question. It was the beauty of New England, and it dwelt as much in delicacy of colour as in the regularity of outline. It was beauty not only of face, but also of figure, as firm, in fact, as it seemed fragile. But perhaps the chief charm lay in the eyes, dreamy yet noble, full of frankness and candour. John Feverel stood before her entranced, or rather as one awakened from reverie to a delightful reality.

As she came toward him, with a brilliant smile of welcome, she held out her hand.

'It is Cousin John, I am sure,' she said. 'Though we did not expect you until to-morrow, I know you. We Feverels are a marked race, with our dark eyes and light hair.'

'And you are Esther?' he said.

'Yes, I am Esther,' was her answer.

The voice was the voice of an angel in its sweetness and purity. John Feverel almost hesitated to believe that he was not dreaming still, that he was no longer peering into the mirror in which he had beheld her only a few minutes before.

'I am sorry that we were not here to welcome you this afternoon, but my father went into town, and I was away in the orchard, and I did not know you were here until I saw your horse.'

He took the hand she extended to him, and murmured inarticulate acknowledgment. He found few words, though he was wont to be ready. His tongue refused its office, but his love spake from his eyes. Her glance fell, under his steady gaze, and a slight blush crimsoned her cheek. It was as though, having seen her once, he did not wish ever again to lose sight of her, and to be compelled to rely on incantation for her reappearance. She hesitated for a little space, and then she continued : 'I hope you will be happy here, as I have been. It is a dear old house, and I have spent my life here, and I love it. But I fear you will not be content with what pleased an ignorant girl, after your wanderings all over the world.'

'What I have seen of the house seems like a glimpse of Paradise,' he said, when at last he found his voice. 'And I should be hard to please if I were to wish to leave it. I am sure that I shall not want to roam again. I shall be content here now ;' and to these last words he gave a deep meaning, so that the blush mantled her cheek again. 'I have come home to rest by my own fireside.'

As he said this she cast an involuntary glance upon the hearth. Then she sprang forward with feverish haste : 'You have let the fire go out,' she said, reproachfully, and it has been burning here day and night, summer and winter, ever since the house was built.'

John Feverel said nothing, but watched her as she heaped the wood over the scant embers and sought to fan them into a flame. Perhaps it was the fixity of his glance which disturbed her, for she arose sharply and turned to seek a match. The skirt of her dress rested for a second on one of the dying embers, and as she stooped again the flames sprang up and enveloped her.

With the prompt decision of a man used to the facing of emergencies, John Feverel seized the heavy Oriental rug which lay before the hearth. He flung it instantly around the girl, and rolled it tightly, extinguishing the slight flame before it had force even to scorch her fair skin. For a minute he kept her wrapped closely in his arms.

Then, as he relaxed his hold a little, she released herself.

' But you must not let the fire go out,' she said, gently, 'even if it did try to burn me.'

He placed her in the chair before the hearth, and he stepped forward and stamped out the last lingering ember, powerless thereafter for good or evil. She watched him with a woman's acquiescence in the force of a man's will. When the last spark was quenched, he came to her and took her hand.

'Let the old fire of intolerance and hatred go out,' he said. 'For nearly two hundred years its smoke has cast a shadow over the Feverels. I hope for a new light and a purer flame on our hearth;' and he knelt beside her, and her hand rested in his.

NEW DOLLAR NOVELS

PUBLISHED BY

CHARLES SCRIBNER'S SONS.

Each One Volume, 12mo Cloth, - - - *$1.00*

VALENTINO.

By *WILLIAM WALDORF ASTOR.*

Price reduced to One Dollar.

A romance founded upon the history of the Borgia family in the early part of the Sixteenth Century, during the lifetime of Pope Alexander VI. and his son Cæsar Borgia. It presents a remarkably carefully studied picture of those stirring times. A story full of spirit and action.

"The details of workmanship are excellent. Mr. Astor writes, apparently, out of a full mind and a thorough interest in his subject."—*Atlantic Monthly.*

"His manner is dignified and his English pleasant and easy."—*Boston Advertiser.*

"It is well called a romance, and no romance indeed could be more effective than the extraordinary extract from Italian annals which it preserves in such vivid colors."—*N. Y. Tribune.*

"A signal addition to the really superior novels of the season."—*The Independent.*

"One cannot read far in 'Valentino' before perceiving that Mr. Astor has written a very creditable romance in the historical field, and one that would not have lacked readers had the name been left off the title."—*N. Y. Times.*

THE LAST MEETING.

By BRANDER MATTHEWS.

Mr. Matthews combines successfully the old style of story, full of plot, and the modern more subtle methods. The *motif* is most original and clear, and at the same time the author shows an uncommon literary dexterity. The scene is laid in New York.

"It is an amusing story and the interest is carried through it from beginning to end."—*N. Y. Times.*

"A wholesome society novel, a strikingly dramatic and thrilling tale, and a tender love story, every word of which is worth reading."—*Critic.*

"A simple but ingenious plot, there is force and liveliness to the narrative, and the pictures of New York social life are done by one 'to the manner born.'"—*Boston Post.*

"A clever and thoroughly original tale, full of dramatic situations, and replete with some new and most expressive Americanisms."—*Literary World.*

WITHIN THE CAPES.

By HOWARD PYLE,

Author of "The Merry Adventures of Robin Hood," etc., etc.

Mr. Pyle's novel is, first of all, an absorbingly interesting one. As a sea story, pure and simple, it compares well with the best of Clark Russell's tales, but it is much more ; the adventures of Tom Granger, the hero, are by no means confined to sea life. Though never sensational, there are plenty of exciting incidents and ever a well-developed mystery. The plot is of the good old-fashioned thrilling sort and the style strong and vigorous.

"Mr. Pyle proves himself a master of nautical technique and an accurate observer. . . . His style is good and fresh, and in its conciseness resembles that of Marryatt."—*N. Y. Journal of Commerce.*

"The style is so quaint, so felicitous, so quietly humorous, that one must smile, wonder and admire."—*Hartford Post.*

A WHEEL OF FIRE.

By ARLO BATES.

Mr. Bates' novel is so unusually strong in its conception that it makes a strong impression on this account alone. It is not only a striking story, but is told with remarkable power and intensity.

"A very powerful performance, not only original in its conception, but full of fine literary art."—*George Parsons Lathrop.*

"One of the most fascinating stories of the year."—*Chicago Inter-Ocean.*

"A carefully written story of much originality and possessing great interest."—*Albany Argus.*

"The plot is clearly conceived and carefully worked out; the story is well told with something of humor, and with a skillful management of dialogue and narrative."—*Art Interchange.*

ROSES OF SHADOW.

By T. R. SULLIVAN.

A most pleasant revival of a type of novel that has been growing rare. A story well told, with the charm of a sincere self-respecting ᵗᵉ that does not lose itself in a search after effects and oddities, and with a strong and healthy plot, not frittered away by perpetual analysis.

"The characters of the story have a remarkable vividness and individuality—every one of them—which mark at once Mr. Sullivan's strongest promise as a novelist. . . . . All of Mr. Sullivan's men are excellent. John Musgrove, the grimly pathetic old beau, sometimes reminds us of a touch of Thackeray."—*Cincinnati Times-Star.*

ACROSS THE CHASM.

A STORY OF NORTH AND SOUTH.

A novel full of spirit and wit which takes up a new situation in American life. The cleverness of the sketching, the admirable fairness of the whole, and a capital plot make the novel one of the brightest of recent years.

"A story which will at once attract readers by its original and striking qualities."—*Journal of Commerce, N. Y.*

"Nothing can be more freshly and prettily written than the last few pages, when Louis and Margaret meet and peace is made. It is a little idyl of its kind. . . . . 'Across the Chasm' not being an impalpable story, but having a live young woman and a live man in its pages, deserves hearty commendation."—*N. Y. Times.*

A DESPERATE CHANCE.

By Lieut. J. D. J. KELLEY, U.S.N.

"A Desperate Chance" is as absorbing as only a novel can be when told with the *verve* of such a writer as Lieut. Kelley. It is a fresh, stirring story, with sufficient adventure, romance and mystery to keep the reader absorbed. It may safely be said that if the tale is once begun it will be finished in a continuous reading, and we think of it as one of the stories we will always remember distinctly, and which was well worth the reading.

"A stirring sea story."—*New York Star.*

" Lieut. J. D. J. Kelley's novel, 'A Desperate Chance,' is of the good old-fashioned, exciting kind. Though it is a sea story, all the action is not on board ship. There is a well-developed mystery, and while it is in no sense sensational readers may be assured that they will not be tired out by analytical descriptions, nor will they find a dull page from first to last."—*Brooklyn Union.*

" 'A Desperate Chance' is a sea story of the best sort. It possesses the charm and interest which attach us to sea life, but it does not bewilder the reader by nautical extremes, which none but a professional sailor can understand. 'A Desperate Chance' reminds us of Mr. Clark Russell's stories, but Lieut. Kelley avoids the professional fault into which Mr. Russell has fallen so often. The book is extraordinarily interesting, and this nowadays is the highest commendation a novel can have."—*Boston Courier.*

COLOR STUDIES.

By T. A. JANVIER (Ivory Black).

A series of most delightful pictures of artists' life in New York which first attracted the attention of readers to Mr. Janvier as a writer of very notable short stories. Certainly among stories dealing with artists' surroundings there have never been written better tales than these which are collected in this beautiful little volume.

"The style is bright, piquant and graphic, and the plots are full of humor and originality."—*Boston Traveler.*

CHARLES SCRIBNER'S SONS,

PUBLISHERS,

743 & 745 Broadway, New York.